AKSHAT KHARE

Akshat Khare is an Indian Novelist and Poet. His experiments with writing and philosophy are directed towards developing a post-postmodern poetics.

Also by Akshat Khare

Delhi Blues and Other Poems
From the Tongue of an Experienced Simpleton
Truth Be Told
The Book of Saudade

Excerpts from this novel appeared in Triple-Ampersand Journal and Deluge Journal.

Signifying Nothing

Akshat Khare

The space of the real

Sometimes I feel that the streets are liquid and if I am not careful, I will end up slipping into the ocean of tarmac and mud that presses against my feet. Heads and faces float on by, followed at some distance by torsos and hands and feet. More and more of them every day.

The birds are beginning to vanish again. The hibiscus that disguises the barbed wire mesh underneath have grown quiet now.

The odd myna still pops its head out before quickly jumping out of view behind the leaves. Only city pigeons are confident enough to strut on the electric wires. The air is becoming visible again. People are waiting for the acid rain. The air will vanish again.

The sharp cold air has a tinge of all-pervading smoke on it. My mind jumps to other balconies and widows that open onto sea air or mountain air.

The paint has dried on the walls of the buildings. They look freshly old and will continue to do so for the next few months provided that the dry spell is not broken in the next few days. The new song picks up and samples an old favourite cool jazz standard before devolving into low-fidelity extended notes and simple beats.

'Karna!'

I steal one last glance at the silent and unmoving hibiscus and remind myself – The birds are beginning to vanish again.

The space of the dream

The old man walks down the streets of the city every day. His movements are slow and he always leans ahead, his left leg dragging behind ever so slightly. The fox that sits on his shoulder is invisible to all – for years, unbeknownst to him the canine has continued to nibble away at the flesh. The arm has lost all movement. But the man is not bothered, he is happy that the arm is still there. It can still be used to fill out sleeves. And sometimes when he's by himself and he is certain that no one else is watching him, he angles the dead arm and leaning his head on it, drifts off to sleep. The red bushy tail of the crafty beast swings from end to end, counting out the hours.

The space of the real

Navya looked up at the sun rising on the concrete cube that was the D.O.M.A. building. The windows caught the early morning light and sparkled.

The air curtain sent her hair in disarray as she walked inside. The click-clack of her heels echoed out in the empty hall. The space was designed to appear warm and inviting, and it did its part in helping D.O.M.A. suck in potential high school and college dropouts when the need for new testers and subjects arose. The dissonance between the modernist exterior and the warm atrium replete with columns and rugs and plush sofas and rounded out surfaces was designed to simultaneously create and alleviate a nervous anxiety that made almost all potential subjects itch to sign up for the program.

'Welcome to the Department of Memetic Archaeology, how may I assist you today?' the glazy eyed receptionist chimed as Navya crossed her desk.

'I've worked here for five years Disha' Navya entered the vestibule without waiting for a response. The receptionist was a former test subject. Any mild annoyance that Navya could have managed would have been beside the point, she had argued against the use of the Discards as clerical workers but the Chief saw it as an effective way to keep tabs on some of the more unreliable and ideation prone subjects.

Her office was at the far end of the east wing. It was a small space, but it was ideally located. She had ready access to the subjects. As she passed the Popcult orientation wings, she eyed the new Dropouts and Hopefuls ready to absorb the Training Materials tailored and designed for the specific niche of their assigned countries and regions.

The large doors of the thousicubular Sweeping Room came into view. Padlocked. Probably with the next shift workers inside already. The end of shift reports would reach her in a few minutes. She braced herself as she made a sharp turn and came to the empty hallway with her office at the end.

The space of the virtual

Archaeology of the memetic artifice rests upon the political dexterity of the species. The metacarpal and the carpal articulate with each other and then with the distal phalanx – these so assembled excavate the endless memetic layers that lay undisturbed. In a single moment the stratigraphical solidity of the artifice is constructed and subsequently but also simultaneously violated, resulting in instant gratification dopamine loops that compel the nameless billion to provide free labour and time to this virtual data mine.

The vitiated thumb regains its vigour after rest or immediately after the removal of the nitrogen bubbles from the joints via osteopathic and mystically gratifying crepitus crackling and popping sensations.

The space of the symbolic

Waltz for the concatenated nothing

Supposing truth were a woman – what then? Inside the ballroom of a fidgety matron with hardwood floors and Viennese chandeliers and décor fit to be present there, designed to bewitch, to mesmerise, to haunt, fascinate and enthral men who wall flowered stand along the walls in their dress shoes waiting for their turn with truth as the quartet plays a waltz. The space was designed to distract these men whose verbose long-winded chatter now peters out against the tall windows and is reduced to an indistinct muffled din whose timbre and tone no longer allow for the reconstruction of the loquacious elocutions that brought them forth. In this largely vacant ballroom, a question often rings out, bouncing around the corners before dissolving into the unventilated sultry air:

Supposing truth were not a woman – what then?

The space of the real

The underground scene in Delhi had evolved but it had not evolved fast enough. At least not in the way Vikram needed it to. Gigabytes of finished footage of his film were gathering virtual dust in the back of some hard drive. The Noise musicians that he could find around the city were less atonal and more tone deaf. Any abandonment of pitch centricity was not the result of a conscious choice but the inevitable generation of random sounds with the misplaced hope that the listeners wouldn't know better. And most of them didn't.

Vikram needed or rather he had hoped to find someone who could play the CRT or a good old label scanner. There was an understandable dearth of CRTelecaster shredders or percussionists for that matter. He had spent the better part of last year shooting footage in alleyways of urban villages in and around the city as the protagonist walked and walked and walked with a Tibetan prayer wheel in his hand, softly rotating it now and then almost without thought, inside the wheel folded pieces of paper that had been carefully sliced out from Marxist-Leninist texts with a thin razor, revolving and multiplying the strength of the sentences; prayers repeated thousandfold. His other hand oscillating between the drag in and breathe out of the plummy Chunghwa cigarettes favoured by Mao himself. Vikram wanted to make a political point, he was not completely decided on what that point was, but he felt that the right piece of music would help him put it all together in the edit.

Vikram really needed Darius to come through for him. There was a prospective candidate who had scored some influencer vids and was supposedly underrated and had a disturbing obsession with Hanatarash. At this point if it was not another washing machine dryer wannabe Avant Garde EDMer, Vikram would take him. He was already anxious about his next project. The need to move on from this and onto something else. But he had to finish this film first. The condensation of time and space rapidly edited into a picture that was taking the shape of The Next Thing inside his mind, but the montage was not tracking a fixed idea and as such might as well have been dismissed out of hand as a daydream. And Vikram would have dismissed it if he had anything better.

The space of the symbolic

At the time on which I have in memory frozen the subject, she hadn't made the jump. Her aesthetic sensibilities or lack thereof quilted around Del Ray and had not devolved or evolved depending on the sympathy or antipathy of the reader with the undercurrents of colonial nostalgia that slips and frets through the grassy hills of the unthinking mind or depending upon the proclivity of the reader towards all things firangi in that realm of Desi that is by necessity a put-on performance that makes alt desi women go from Del Ray to Madhubala and sometimes back the other way.

Any performance that the performer leans into sincerely blurs the fine line between the idiosyncrasies of the character and those of the performer, making it impossible for them and the audience to tell where the person ends and where the performance begins leading to that grey place where foibles of the persona are indistinguishable from the quirks that take a lifetime to cultivate.

A drape of that Schopenhauerian sadness that veils an ego that rests firmly on an edifice of half-read books, cigarettes and candy store variety of nihilism that is never in short supply falling over the shoulder in shiny liquorice black waves of hypnotizing hair.

The space of the real

Where was it? Alessandro had seen it peripherally. But he was certain he had seen it in his feed. The auto-refresh had removed it before he could get at it. He felt the bile rise in his mouth. There was nothing he could do but wait. He cracked his neck twice and went back to the codex. The text was charting out the creation of alkahest in its first layer, but it was the deconstructive reading that interested him. Open on the table for reference was Nagarjuna's Rasendra Mangalam and Bacon's Instauratio Magna. Every word that passed under his eye was fuelling his ever-increasing suspicion that the code was designed to lead nowhere or worse to the creation of fulminating gold that would explode midway through the experiment. The adepts had conspired against him. Against all of them. The old masters he could forgive but the new ones, the accelerationists he couldn't. The texts resisted fracturing. He looked out of the window. The sunlight would soon be gone. He made a new category in his Zairja and noted the resulting combinations down. Outside the warm Adriatic air was washing over the streets of his maze-like town. The last few weeks had been tortuous. Alessandro felt like he was snatching at something that was always out of his grasp. The image that came in and out of his feed but never stayed. The texts almost made sense but then they didn't. The more he pulled at the threads the tighter the weave held the secrets together. The adepts were known to passively misguide seekers but would they actively target him? The Rosicrucian order was long dead. The A.M.O.R.C.s then? Doubtful. Someone was behind it. It was clear how they had identified that he was looking in the right place. Ever since he had contacted the translator, things hadn't gone his way. The translation of the codices from ancient Sanskrit to Italian wouldn't have been hard to trace. The need for textual clarity had driven him to ruin. He was certain of it. They knew. They knew. The elusive meme that resisted seeing. It was them. He was sure of it. He had to capture more and more of the image in his memory as it came his way. The meanings coded in it were his only way forward. The only thing that could help him arrest the spread of the disease. Signs. Signifiers. Floating away from him. Resisting. Something had to be done. The books were a dead end. The image then had to be a new door. Maybe he had spent all his life opening doors looking for the prima materia, not for once ceasing to stop in his search through Zawgyi texts, Rasashatric codices, faux Grimoires, all on paper, while behind him the exit waited patiently. The virtual had to be his way out. The sunlight finally went out. The lamps threw the shapes of his ornate window grills against his ceiling. His cell phone still on the table washed the paper and wood around it in its white glow. The feed kept auto-refreshing but the meme did not appear again. It was only a matter of time he decided. A few more days and he would see its totality. There was no rush. He had struggled for years, what difference would a few more weeks make? He reached out to the phone and fixed his eyes on the feed.

The space of the dream

'I' enters the room. 'I' sees a man on the hospital bed. The smell of disinfectant pierces the air. The white clean tiles soft and inviting stand in stark contrast against the pale-yellow linens of his bed sheet. Masses of necrotic flesh stick out in gooey patches on his arms and legs and chest. The man sniffs and corrects his hospital gown. 'I' runs out in horror. 'I' leaves the sanitised lights of the ward and runs up the spiralling staircase, 'I's hand is bleeding now from the rust of the cast iron railings. 'I' does not let go. 'I' does not dare look back. 'I' keeps running up the endless staircase. The oxygen thins out. 'I' feels their teeth fall out, one by one, clattering in the dark down the endless staircase. The ring of dull calcium coated with plaque incisors and molars against the hospital marble punctuates the empty. 'I' feels around their mouth – the tongue reaches out and touches the soft tissue that had held the orthodontic artifice in place, 'I' doesn't break pace. 'I' keeps running. 'I' doesn't look back.

Look back.

The space of the real

The letter had shown up on his doorstep like an uninvited guest. And it was in his nature to be ill-disposed to people and things he had invited into his life. To be charitable to something or someone that had shown up unbidden was unthinkable. It had been sitting there in the hallway, alone and waiting instead of his morning newspaper. He brushed the symbol on the envelope lightly with his thumb as he picked it up. The snake emblazoned on it was biting its own tail. Pavan stepped back inside with the parcel dangling between the tips of his fingers.

He was confronted by the foul smell of his apartment. Three minutes of fresh air in the hallway had served to cleanse his nasal palate. He moved slowly towards his chair, his nose adapting to the surroundings with every step. Pavan slumped in his chair and put his feet on the table. He wondered why he felt this miserable this early in the morning. He looked at the envelope once again. The red ink of the Ouroboros flared menacingly against the empty white space of the eggshell white cardstock paper. Pavan's gaze moved to the sheets of paper on his desk. Three lines on an otherwise empty page stared back at him defiantly. He let out a deep sigh and read the sentences, sounding them out inside his head as his eyes moved across the irregular rises and falls of his own handwriting. Three sentences, Pavan thought to himself. A day's work. He wondered if it would not have been better to not have worked at all yesterday.

Behind the pages, paperbacks and hardcovers of varying thicknesses, patterns and severity were stacked precariously, and would have come tumbling down if Pavan ever opened the windows, which he never did. Next to them his thesaurus and his language dictionaries lay open on top of each other. The ends of his life had begun to unravel, fraying out one after the other. He could feel them tugging at him in all directions, slowly pulling him apart. Pavan worked as a translator. He worked as seventeen translators to be precise. He had fabricated seventeen different people with various specialisations. Work was hard to come by, and the pseudonyms ensured that he had something or the other to do even as the demand for one thing dwindled or the competition for another saturated. An old man who worked only with Urdu and English, a young novelist who specialised in Haikus, an autodidact who had taught herself Italian and worked with post war writers, a middle aged mother of two who updated nineteenth century translations of Latin texts, a mathematician who translated mathematical pamphlets from Hindi into English, a part time content writer who worked exclusively with pulp romances, another who dealt only with mystery fiction, a greying business man who proofed young adult fiction, a student who had completed her thesis on largely forgotten French feminist writers, three sisters who worked with eastern bloc anti-communist literature having lost their father in the invasion of Hungary, a young man who worked with German writers who were suppressed by the Nazis, a retired academic who having run out of books he wanted to read now compiled the 'Best translated literature of the year' lists for magazines, a leftist who made Latin American writers accessible to the masses in regional languages, another who worked with queer literature and lastly a thirty three year old man who translated graphic novels or comic books, depending on your linguistic preferences.

Pavan carried all of them with him and could feel them sometimes falling over and pushing around in his head. But they had no real existence. They were just names that had captured certain characteristics or others from the floating sea of signifiers. They were creations of convenience that he maintained through a complex network of friends and agents. He would not have pulled any of them out of non-existence had the fad for specialists not been the defining market factor of the zeitgeist. He did not speak most of the languages he worked with and had formal training in only two or three of them. He made up for this with a rich stock of dictionaries, phrasebooks, and the internet. He kept up with various forums and was more than happy to delegate the work to helpful native speakers online.

Translation, Pavan thought to himself was supposed to be his tertiary pursuit. But it had ended up being his primary source of income. He had moved to Delhi to write novels. Regrettably for him, the writing of novels and the publishing of novels were two distinctly different endeavours. In the last year or so, after re-reading his first novel several times, he had to face the inescapable conclusion that it was terrible and derivative. And with each passing day, his desire to put it out became more diminished until it was just a little flicker in the back of his mind, sustained by nothing but his insecurity and his ego.

His fingers moved with a mind of their own and began picking expertly at the flaps of the envelope. His secondary pursuit was perhaps the one that depressed him more than the respective successes and failures he had had with the other two. An old friend who worked in publishing had convinced him to become one of the ghostwriters who kept up the Allen Kaufman detective stories that put out eight titles out every year. He wasn't interested in working with pulp fiction but it allowed him to exercise his writing muscles. Or at least that was how he chose to justify it to himself. He often ended up plagiarizing bits and pieces of Christie or Simenon or Chandler shuffling and jumbling them together until they stopped being Christie, Simenon and Chandler and became instead the style with which the pseudonym had been writing for eighty years now. He pulled out the single sheet of paper from inside the envelope and flattened it out against the uneven surface of the desk. The page was typed with a typewriter. Pavan traced out the ink that had been pressed into the paper. The cream stock had aged with some foxing around the edges, as if it had been passed through too many hands and had been looked at by too many eyes.

It was gibberish.

The letters alternated between Cyrillic and Arabic. They had been typed out with two different typewriters, Pavan hazarded. He looked at his Hermes sitting obediently in the corner waiting for a second novel that would never come. He kept it clean by dusting it regularly, but the harder to clean edges had accumulated the archaeological record of disuse in layers of dust. Pavan looked at the page. He turned it over in his hand carefully, examining the impression that the alphabets had left on the paper. The pages looked too elaborate to be a prank. He pulled out some fresh sheets and started copying down the alternating alphabets on different pages. He uploaded the Arabic to a forum of polyglots who had coalesced around their love for Ibn Rushd, the Cyrillic he texted over to his online friend.

He could have compared the alphabets to keys on the internet, but it was simply quicker to let the natives sort it out. The invisible horde of translators were there at his fingertips, waiting to be summoned like Djinns who volunteered their services purely out of their love for helping strangers across the internet. All translators were invisible in a way. So were ghostwriters. He wondered who was more invisible. Ghostwriters were paid to stay hidden. Good translators practiced self-erasure, the best translations naturally being the ones that contained everything of the writer and nothing of the translator; thieves in the night wiping out their footprints from the texts as they overturned it and dragged it from its native tongue firmly into an alien one. When he was just starting out, Pavan felt a nervous sort of excitement when he spotted people reading things that he had translated, he looked at the titles and the people who had their noses buried in them. He had felt the urge to walk over and casually ask them if they were enjoying themselves. But he couldn't get his body to move. It was the first time Pavan had realised what was now a firm and mapped out philosophy; Translators were not accorded the same privilege as writers. No one wants to be interrupted in their reading by a translator. No one fantasises about meeting the translator of one volume or another – except perhaps other translators, some academics and a handful of pedants, the latter two often being mutually inclusive.

He shrugged off the soft layer of gloom that was slowly beginning to descend on him and checked his phone. Someone had translated the texts. Pavan reached for a pencil and started copying out the alphabets. The room was unnaturally silent, punctuated only by the scratching of the graphite against the grain of the paper. As he put down the final alphabets, he looked at the mess which had no discernible meaning. He grabbed the original sheet, and compared it to the other two he had ended up with. Pavan wrote out the alphabets, alternating the translated ones as the original did.

He read out the first line. But the line under that had no

meaning, incoherent and coherent words came one after the other finally ending in the middle after which the page dissolved into an absolute lack of discernible meaning once again. Pavan looked at the page impatiently and wondered if the whole thing was simply designed to waste his time. He focused on the page and traced out the complete string of sentences he could find. Eventually, he spotted more phrases spread out across the page, vertically and then in horizontal reversals before the pattern finally revealed itself to him all at once.

He slowly and carefully traced out the spiral into which the letters were falling. He followed the curve before finally making its way to the very centre – revealing the story at the heart of the labyrinth.

The space of the virtual

He looked at the stats for THE CASK, one of the several groups he modded on Philbook. There was an exponential rise in engagement and page views but he hadn't noticed any increase in the number of reacts or comments. This clearly pointed to the rise of lurkers who were observing the going-ons inside the group but were choosing not to participate. Not that he was looking forward to modding pseudposts and the same carousel of the endless starter phil. 101s and edgy ultra-ironic takes, but an increase in participants sans interactions generally didn't bode well for most groups.

The space of the dream

In a warm yellow lit café with missing windowpanes in the hills of the Himalayas – people are sitting looking out of the door – waiting on someone. The red bike parked outside has a light dusting of snow, the corvette cooled waits for them to take it back home. On the crossroads where one hill cuts into another a man in a long trench coat is adjusting his false teeth and readying his trumpet. The wild-eyed ghost watching him from the shadows wistfully checks his empty case; wind passing through lungs that cannot draw breath. The music flows a little before losing itself in the pines and the stillness of the night.

The space of the real

His breath was fogging up the glass. Karna looked at the road passing under him, rippling, and changing now like a river, now like the strings of a harp. He had put his book away and was pretending to be asleep. One of his batchmates had just gotten on and he had no desire to speak or be spoken to.

His Tech classes ended up being the longest commute of them all because they had no Metro connectivity. It gave him time to recover from the first two-thirds of his day. Karna liked buses more than the metro because of the privacy. It was harder for people to look at each other inside buses. No need to keep up any pretences. No need to impress any strangers with how you hold yourself. There were days when the endless travel and commute to different classes on different campuses got to him. But these fluctuations were separated by enough days in between them for him to not be perturbed by them. His disdain was too general to be of any consequence to himself or to the world around him. He knew that he shouldn't give in to the institutionalised apathy. But he just couldn't bring himself to care anymore. He was at the end of his string. Most of the people he knew were at the end of theirs. The evening circles didn't help as much as they used to. It was just more work and more commute. It had been almost three years since the new education act had been passed into legislation and forced down the throats of all the states one way or another. If you didn't spend enough time with the same people then you wouldn't organise them politically. The months that followed had seen a contrary effect. But now that some years had passed, the long game was lost. Not much had changed either. The absence of an aggravating opposition hadn't led to fascism, but to more of the same as before, the same slow march to extinction that they had been on for quite some time even before the act had been a draft on some inconsequential minister's desk.

The space of the dream

He started walking along the narrow alleys, looking at the wares, his palms itching; he shoved his hands inside his coat pocket and started rubbing the coins in there to ease his nervousness. A stranger patted him on the shoulder.

'Heard you're looking for a typewriter.'

'What's it to you?'

'You'll find one there.' The man pointed with his unclean thumb. He started following him, finding himself in front of a dark old building in an alleyway around a corner that nobody turns. He climbed the staircase, his heart beating tentatively, racing in anticipation. This was the real high, everything after this was just a formality. He went through it because it was a part of the game and nothing more. The man was waiting for him, standing at the door of a dinghy little room. He stepped inside and could feel the man's eyes following him as he made his way across the room.

'So where is it?' he asked. He couldn't see it anywhere. The man pointed at the brown cloth that was draped over the box next to him. He lifted it off in one swift movement.

And there it was . . . a Clark Nova. At last. After decades. Decades. Here he was, and here it was. 'How much?' he asked. But he didn't need to know, it didn't matter to him. He saw the pusher sharpening his teeth in the corner as he stepped out of the building. He was quietly standing there, file to teeth, humming a tune. He picked up the tune and carried it all around the city as he traced his way back home. Clutching the Clark Nova securely in his hands. He could taste it in his mouth, the overpowering taste of him placing the Clark Nova in his collection. He held on to the feeling strongly all day. On the bus, on the metro, the flight and the metro and the bus again. His mind revolved around all the highlights of his long career. The satisfaction of holding his first Olivetti Valentine as the dusty poplars were shaking in the wind. The ant colony that had been living inside his Hermes 3000, and the clear clean pleasure of exterminating them.

What about her? Surely, he must tell her that he was out of the typewriter game. Just as she was out of the painting game for good. He had seen to that, hadn't he now? He would tell her as soon as he found the correct place for the Clark Nova. They could be happy together now that they were both out. He turned the key and opened the door. She was there. Waiting for him.

The walls were dripping with black ash mixed with red paint.

It oozed out of the cracks in the plaster and was coagulating as it made its way down to the floor. His eyes ran over the walls before slowly coming to rest on the behemoth that occupied the centre of his rooms. There were fractals in there that his brain just could not process. She had taken them apart. All of them. Platens, Knobs, Keys, Spools. It was all assembled into this large sculpture of a woman. Archetypical with eight hands ending in thin fingertips that were made out of the key levers. The cover plates were repurposed as clavicles – three sets of trunks made from the mesh of countless machines and the eyes, oh the eyes, glowing red-orange in the darkness – spool covers from his Olivetti Valentines.

He glared at her, marvelling as she sat there insolently, slender throat, eyes sparkling, his fingers loosened around the Clark Nova as she wet her lips. He walked over to her, as she swung her legs from the divan and moved to make some space for him. 'It is only fair you know' she said, fixing her dark eyes on him. 'It is. It is.' he nodded his head, his eyes still running over the sculpture. She put her arms around him as he sat down to look at the monstrosity she had begotten.

The space of the real

'If that isn't poetry in motion then what is.'

'I don't catch your drift, Mr. Brown'

'Look at the man, look how he swings through space. The movements of the brush, the synchronicity of the roller with the wall, and the colour traced out in the wake of his passing.'

'What of his assistant then?'

'A minor blip at the edge of the canvas Mr. White, No one sees the sketch lines'

The wall painter is swinging by a thin bungee line and is sitting on a frayed and grimy polyester blue harness – the other worker pushes him out and pulls him in – running down to the balconies of the floors below him as the painter slowly lowers himself with a bright red jumar. He is on the eighteenth floor right now.

'Space is meant to be traversed. Don't you ever feel frustrated by the Cartesian restrictions placed on man?'

'Not Euclidean ones?'

'Non-Euclidean but restricted to the surface in one way or the other.'

'To what end?'

'To the other side of a Mobius Strip.'

'I see.'

'But look at the assistant, surely his presence is a great comfort; a definite stopper to the pendulous swing of the painter.'

The wall painter and his assistant are on the sixteenth floor now. Sitting on the balcony, smoking.

'I do so despise time theft.'

'Ontologically?'

'No. These endless breaks that the workers take – chatting, smoking. Look at them sprinkling their ashes on our heads.'

'Culture, Mr. White, can't be expected from the noble savages.'

The wall painter is waiting on the fourteenth-floor's balcony. His assistant is mixing the paint in the PVC bucket.

'At the preconscious level, all space is openness, Mr. Brown.'

'And all being thrownness.'

'Isn't that an antiquated notion?'

'There is nothing new under the sun.'

The sun is biting the painter's neck as he paints the edge of the twelfth floor; the sweat from his eyebrows is stinging his eyes.

'The viscosity of the liquid, how do you think they adjust that without knowing?'

'I remember a little of the formula. It was Nu wasn't it?'

'Either Nu or Mu. Something or the other.'

'It's all an approximation with their work. The builders advertise scientific techniques, but it is all unsupervised rule of thumb when it comes to the actual work.'

'You get what you pay for I suppose.'

The workers are discussing their dinner as they cover the tenth-floor balcony. The week is at its end, so either chicken or fish – but which?

'You know Mr. White, Sometimes I look at the endless reproduction of these buildings and wonder why they aren't better designed. If I didn't know better, I would say the architects were plagiarising the brutalists or at least had some unsavoury spatial notions in their heads.'

'It comes with the territory. There are only so many ways they can carve out the land before it gets repetitive again. I am sick of those new-fangled glass monstrosities with curves and loops and missing spaces in between them.'

The painter is trying to reach out to a far-away patch on the eighth floor. He stretches out the roller – his arm sinewy and strained.

The bungee line snaps.

The space of the symbolic

When philosophers and academics use an old word in a new sense to cut open the fabric of signification hoping to open new meanings distinct from those close but distinct shades that were claimed by their predecessors – are they pulling the wool over our eyes? Is our intuitive grasp on the sudden unconcealedness of this new shade of meaning an actual event or are we just convincing ourselves that the shadows cast against the walls are men with intentionality?

The space of the real

He cracked his neck and walked into the room. There were forty or fifty students his age scattered around the lecture hall. Karna spotted Vikram in the corner fiddling with his Bolex and threw himself into the seat next to him. He half nodded and half looked up to acknowledge Karna's presence, his hands fiddling with the lenses. There was no point in talking to him when he was assembling or disassembling his equipment.

The doors in the front simultaneously flew open as Professor Surf and Professor Turf barged in from the left and the right, flourishing their gowns as they walked amongst the students.

Turf began 'To accelerate the contradictions to the singularity is the sole purpose of this seminar.'

Surf followed 'The contradictions in capital that fester need skilled surgeons who are unafraid to dive into the mess.'

'The constant refusals of the governments to let the free markets have their reign are what is halting the procession to the singularity.' Turf articulated bringing his fingers closer together and then suddenly yanking them apart.

'It is the need of the hour that we see the failures of organisation within our ranks, and our inability to repel the tentacles of pomo late melancholy capitalism that have led to the rise of the global right.' Surf nodded his head.

'I see men hunting deer in the ruins of Lutyens. After the collapse of the singularity in on itself – only an unflinching breakneck push to the far right will bring us to the post-scarcity haven.' Turf waved his hand in a stylised fashion.

Karna stifled a yawn as the two men moved schizophrenically through the classroom. The Point-Counterpoint style was a staple of their lectures. Dialectic teaching had started out as a fringe style in the humanities Unis before invading their way into the sciences since the new education act had been passed. The simuloteach of String Theory with Loop Quantum Gravity, the rise and fall of the Reich with the rise and fall of the Soviets, and so on. The pedagogic roots of the form had been a distinct invention of the metropol, the establishment had seamlessly appropriated and now it was being used in the consistent production of radical centrists.

Turf boomed 'The nightmare breathes out from the signifiers you have buried it under. Unfettered its fingers will reach out and strangle the petty unionists and welfarists. Already the socius sees itself moving in a being-towards-death as salarymen die from overwork, the machine churns and the incline to the pure rhizome of the capital accelerates.'

'The disappointments of the last century and the immense failure of alternatives to an authoritarian solution leaves us only with the praxis of interrupting flows. The jarring of the machine as it turns, a deceleration is the left-handed monkey wrench that will jam the assemblage.' Surf sighed.

Nitish quietly moved his phone under his bag as Turf passed him, resuming the stream of amateur porn as Turf moved towards the stage – the philanthropic gesture was the subject of Vikram's cinephile blog last month on ways of seeing and sharing films. Karna suspected that the Profs knew. Either they allowed it because they felt it added to the lecture content or they genuinely didn't care.

'The zombie moves through the cyclical day and repeats . . . .'

'. . . . the vampiric fangs sink in and bleed dry the proletariat'

Zaheer was doomscrolling again. Karna could see his thumb moving automatically without pausing. The posts registering in a continuum on the back of his eyelids, Akhil was penning furiously in coded red and blue inks. A small group was rolling joints in the back while passing around the new smokeless vape 2000.

'The rising share of Conke in the market, the inviting red and white curved lettering . . .'

'. . . Bepis' attempts to copyright local potatoes were thankfully halted by the judiciary.'

The dialectic was in motion by being still. Vikram was scribbling in his Kitchen-sink Film folder now and had put away the Bolex.

'The circulatory function can be reformatted for cyberspace. The flow of the market can surge, and the surplus that recreates itself can move the stats forward.' Turf had opened a magazine and was reading it as he went on. 'The active redirection and redefinition of individual libidos into the sped up roided economy. . .'

Surf was morosely staring out of the window watching the sunlight filter through the old banyan outside 'The Kyberspace's distribution of energies along the rhizomatic channels can be used to take down the hegemony that the oligarchy enjoys. A duct-taped cobbled together war machine that aims itself against the uno percento.'

Turf tossed the stress ball he had been frantically squeezing to Surf who caught it without looking. 'The cold reptilian nature of the text moves within the reconstructive dynamic avoiding both the formal conservatism of the formal sciences and the material conservation of dogmatic metaphysics.' Turf attacked.

'The zombified flesh of the commuter caught in the tangle of the semiotic parasites. The hypnagogic drift lures the signifiers in where they are caught unawares.' Surf parried.

'Oriental modes of non-being signal the decay . . . .'

'Occidental theopolitics functions on the repression . . . .'

Karna could see Akhil was about to reach his breaking point. The ink was flying out from the chewed-out ends of both his pens. The stress ball was flying across the room as the two sparred/lectured on. Some people had fallen asleep on their desks, and the faint smell of marijuana was enveloping the back benches. Latecomers had snuck in and were trying to catch the train crash of thought that was the seminar.

Turf put the stress ball on the lectern and began in an affected voice 'The medico-military complex seizes on the bodies of the Other and reanimates the deadened impulses, waiting for the pointers to move and the graphing needle to violently oscillate. In suburbia, the legislated silence marks the snatching of forms and shapes from unsuspecting corners. When the pupil dilation of the unresponsive twitches, so does the shadow of the superstructure. Tiny flicks on the edges of an endless monolith. Where do you go from there?'

'Inside the Vampire Castle, the bidding of the bloodsuckers is coded, decoded, and then recoded into the fabric of our lives. Outside those gates, Trolls bang their heads against the walls, out of a dissatisfaction born from the absence of truth and justice. The din drowns itself out and the stones drink in the sound as the castle stands unshaken. The deniers of the myth lead as its arch-priests and the flesh on plastic that graphs out language on the memory drive is an endless performance between man and machine. Where do we go from here?' Surf sighed.

'Paths open up through the maze and the tendrils of the potent try to reterritorialize when any attempts are made to disrupt the privatization of desire in the localized regions of operation.'

'The people trapped inside an empty mall haunted by the clicks of heels that echo against the marble while store announcements and spaced-out music flows through the empty. At the centre of an abysmal labyrinth, the mall outside which endless sweatshops churn out the thingamajigs that populate the shelves and the endless floodlit aisles of product.'

Vikram tapped Karna on his shoulder and turned him onto the livestream of a speed chess game that was taking place in row five. The campus was being swept up in Hypermodern Revivalism and Player1 was attacking like an early Alekhine. Player2 was moving more deliberately like a late Lasker. The pessimist streak in his pawn sacrifices was unmistakeable. The Reti opening by the white was quickly devolving into a tied up middle game. Player1 was edging towards a pawn and rook ending but Player2 wasn't having any of it and was on the cusp of forcing an exchange.

'The anorganic functionalism that dissolves all schizoanalytical questions – that fractures in the machine unconscious' flux – that disrupts the directional flows – that short circuits the nomadic controls – that opens invasive channels – that formats the domain – that misdirects the trajectories – that plucks the gloomy hermeneutical vein from within the tangled vessels – that decelerates to the cybernegative – that derides the precedents with a cold-blooded humour – that deploys the quantitative implosion – that disassembles the integrated systems of control – that breaches the boundaries of the virtualized real – that disactualizes the productive force of the emotive quotient – that dehumanises the convergence of automated tendencies – that dismantles the syncopated space – that undoes the reterritorialization.'

Black's last move is apparently very clever as he has won a rook and his menacing Queen is still guarded. But after White's move, the bubble bursts. There is a concentrated hunt on Blacks' King. The double mate threat is renewed and it is forcing Black's reply. White sacrifices its last knight; the rook cannot be captured with a check. Poetry.

'And so the loss of faith in the earliest interpretations of the methodology of the sign is taken up and so the originary trauma of the being is suppressed through repetition and so the space that curves around desire is warped and is the shortest path to through the field and so the instrumentalism of the hyper-affluent and the bored denizens leads to empty inclusiveness and so eruption of vicious boredom is interrupted and so the stirred up discontent froths over and so the ideolog-ical gains are outstripped and taken over and so antagonism regains ground over faux politeness and so the catalytic role of the people in defecting from a regressive futurism is invigorated and so on and so on'

Discover Check.
Black Resigns.

A second game had begun but Karna couldn't be bothered to follow it. The Professors are speeding up now. He can't keep up with the volley of exchanges. A few students are pouring in from some other dismissed class and are slowly inching toward the primordial pull of the two men.

'The celebreality is bred or to be more precise it is fed into a positive feedback loop that centres the consciousness of the self. The comforting and harmless reflection of the mediocre minor celeb is contrasted against the mediocre reflection of the self that comforts and is so to say fangless. In this infernal meld of performativity, the narcotic is no longer junk, it is the person themselves.' Surf turned sharply.

Turf moved against him swiftly, almost colliding 'The soul stealing nanotechnics invade and hack the cyberconscious and disrupt the flows of anti-production leading to synthetic thought control in overdrive.'

'The technihilo move of the feed that refreshes eternally generates new possibilities and lines of flight. The flesh-wire tendrils of postmodernity eke out of the silicon-glass and wraps itself around the neck of the user. The laminar flow goes undisturbed and any turbulence is erased from the matrix of the signifiers.' Their movements were becoming more animated by the minute. They were quickly pacing the breadth of the room – switching with each other as they passed each other in the centre.

'The carcass of the social strata is ripe for infestation by the maggots of inefficiency. To slow down is death. The vaporizers of the future await the sacrifice of the present in factories that dole out bits and pieces of what is to come on the perpetual conveyer belt.' Turf dabbed at the sweat on his brow absentmindedly.

There was a dark look on Surf's face. He was striding towards the window with downcast eyes. He looked at the clouds moving against the sun and turned back to the students. His eyes were gleaming out from under his heavy eyebrows 'The interactions of the subjects that have been reduced to a flux of frozen images will be the very tool of its awakening. The contradictions will implode and the striated space will become smooth.'

The men stopped pacing around the stage and finally came to a stop in the centre of the room with a flourish of their gowns. They tilted their heads in a faux bow just as the bell began to ring overhead. A small crowd peeled off from the people leaving the lecture and closed in around the professors in a tight circle. The voices of the students hovered around the two men for a moment before dissolving into a flurry of self-satisfied murmurs. Vikram and Karna were the first ones out of the lecture hall.

The space of the virtual

The recent splits in Leftbook hadn't come as a surprise to anyone. Some would even say they were long overdue. At least Hoxhaist and Trotskyist infighting in the comment sections was at its end. One of the splinter groups had devolved into pure idpol neolibs who were excited to be enslaved by the admin and were ready to lick his virtual feet for the clout that would come with mod-dom of the group. There was a brief attempt at a truce by the Tankies and the Castroists but fundamental ideological differences over the Spanish Civil War made any attempts at reconciliation impossible.

The space of the real

The Chief was breathing down on her neck.

It was clear to all parties present in the Cylinder what was riding on the success of the experiment. The Vehicle had signed all his release forms and was strapped into the gyro-chair. Navya was throwing out instructions to the techs as they triple checked the wave function monitors. She threw an assuring smile at the subject and signalled the techs to leave.

'How are we feeling today?' she gently placed her hand on his and closed her fingers softly around his wrist. 'A-Okay Doc' he smiled. She noticed that some of his teeth were crooked.

'We'll just run the sim and have you out in a few minutes', she added cloyingly, trying to focus anywhere else but his teeth.

The Chief had already left the Cylinder. As she entered the observation area, she noted that there was an air of unease and uncertainty. The new crop of interns were checking their notes and shifting about behind the Chief.

Behind the plate glass, the repli-modules were beginning to stream on the HD TV sets around the circumference of the room. The chair slowly began to turn on its axis. A thousand chattering Ugandan Knuckles appeared on the dozen TVs placed around the Cylinder – overlapping cries of 'do you know de wey' echoed around the room. The chair began to gain angular velocity. The subject was smiling confidently, sharply turning his head like a ballerina in order to not get dizzy. There were sounds of furious note taking behind Navya as the interns noted down the rising levels of dopamine and endorphins in the Vehicle.

All twelve screens began to play old memes, and a schizoid rush of footage flashed across the different screens. Jump scares from the 2010s spliced in with pink guy videos played on one screen, 8-bit vid reacts videos on played another, and two screens kept alternating between shock vids and snuff films. The subject looked unfazed. Navya looked to the Chief to see if he wanted to escalate. The man was scratching his chin thoughtfully and after what felt like an eternity he nodded. The stream changed – twelve stand-ups simultaneously launched into their sets. "What's the deal with decaf?" "I'm afraid of getting married man" "You know how when you've got a phrase you're not meant to say?" "Alright here's the story, I can remember it like it was yesterday" "There's a big debate about sick jokes" "Well we like war, we're a warlike people" "I had a hotdog for breakfast today" "Comedy, Hunh. We're really doing it folks." "I don't get the paper much anymore" "How come nothing good ever happens at work?" "It's good to be here, It gives me a reason to get out of the house" "No I promise continuity, I'll behave myself. I'll do all the lines that we rehearsed, you know" The subject's mouth was beginning to contort into an unnatural smile. Navya watched the man's appearance change as the chair's rotation increased. His face was turning into a blur of his features. There was a single black line where his eyebrows used to be, his ears and nose were an ill-defined blur but his grin hung back in the air unmoving and disembodied. The Chief took out a small pad and made some observatory notes in it. Navya deescalated the streams and the rotation and monitored his vitals. As the chair came to a stop, two techs unfastened the latches and the man fell out of the chair and promptly vomited on the floor.

The janitorial crew solemnly entered the room with their industrial strength chemicals.

The space of the symbolic

Variations on Discipline and Punishment

Is it surprising that prisons resemble factories, factories resemble schools, schools resemble military barracks, military barracks resemble hospitals, hospitals resemble post offices, post offices resemble judicial courts, judicial courts resemble museums, museums resemble police stations, police stations resemble corporate offices, corporate offices resemble pig sties, pig sties resemble zoos, zoos resemble parliament, parliament resemble banks, banks resemble mortuaries, mortuaries resemble malls, malls resemble parking lots, parking lots resemble immigration departments, immigration departments resemble supermarkets, supermarkets resemble psych wards, psych wards resemble labs . . . which all resemble prisons?

The space of the virtual

The virtual retrospective had taken months to put together. Had they gone with the search stats it would have been easier. However the admins agreed that their content needed that personal touch for their t-shirt business to be a success. The Philosophers Collective was one of the oldest groups on Philbook. The Admins and the Mods had a lot riding on the success of the exhibition.

The K-space was the brainchild of one of the nouveau art collectives that were trying to revive Futurism. The project was D.O.A., but the timely arrival of a global pandemic had saved them and launched their gallery to the forefront of the analog to digital shift. The aesthetics were a mesh of early modernist and vaporwave sensibilities. Inside the space, sounds were simulated with the proper echo shifts and reverbs. And the audio tour allowed for a wide range retrowave selection to further heighten the ambience. For people who owned sufficiently advanced VR headsets complete with haptics and airsims the k-space was primed with customisable textures and airflows.

The default stale air with 45% humidity wasn't for everyone. The central staircase spiralled all the way to the top, moving chronologically forward with the elevation. Near the entryway timeless classics like 'All Your Base Are Belong to Us' and 'The Last Page of the Internet' were reverentially housed in small alcoves with plaques. As the visitors made their way to the first floor, 'O Rly', 'Edge', 'Nevada -Tan', 'Gaijin 4Koma', 'Rules of the Internet' and other classics from the mid-noughts greet-ed the eye. And as one progressed the transition to the late noughts snuck up suddenly with 'Boxxy' and 'Creepy-Chan.' A discreet corridor led to the restrooms and unsurprisingly to the scatological exhibits. The second floor was dedicated solely to rage comics and here is where there was a break in the strict chronology with the late Wojak emote renditions of the rage emotes, juxtaposed for effect. The third floor was three times the size of the first two and wouldn't be architecturally feasible outside of cyberspace. The boom of the memes in the opening of the twenty-tens demanded discernment on the part of curators, and some difficult decisions had to be made.

The Collective hoped to make bank with 'Mega Milk' tee sales, and further hoped to tap into the Incel market with prints of 'Rule 34' and the 'Navy Seals Copypasta'. The whole fifth floor was dedicated to 'Pepe' and would also be a big money maker. The fourth floor was dedicated to 'Doge' and had an alternate entry way that allowed Users to enter directly and then restricted them to the meta-ironic wholesomeness of the meme.

The sixth and the seventh floors covered the end of the twenty-tens and the opening of the twenties. The sixth floor had its focus on the more absurdist trends like 'Loss,' 'Ligma,' 'E' and 'Big Chungus'. While the seventh and final floor leaned more towards YT content creators and Tiktokers.

The new laws had put some restrictions on the use of memes for merch, and as a result, most of the exhibits were co-owned by the creators. While they had to take a hit on the profits, the promotion of their own exhibits by influencers was guaranteed to bring their loyal fan bases to the store. Kat, Belle, and Ricardo were slated to make guest appearances.

Unbeknownst to the Collective, the members of Accelerationism Incorporated were closely monitoring the retrospective.

XLR8

The Notebook of Disquiet
Thursday April 12th 2027
Categories: Codex 779

"I am sick of everything, and of the everythingness of everything."

-Pessoa

The furore over the lost notebooks of Dr. Hamid Parsani refuses to die out. There are rumours of a lost notebook that has surfaced in the streets of Mumbai. Having followed the footsteps of Sadeq Hedayat, Parsani found himself on the shores of the Mayanagri looking for respite from the people who were behind his research. The contents of the notebook are unknown, but if the past is an indication, it is in the best interest of the Shah's regime and the petrobarons of India to ensure the papers never see the light of day. I think of Pessoa's trunk and the notes that would have been forgotten and lost to time had someone not stumbled upon them. Seeing the endless combinations that the texts lend themselves to, one is almost tempted to say they came from the alchemists. I do not believe that one single work can accelerate us to the singularity, but the assemblages that can be formed out of them will lead to a hyperstitial confluence that will turn the tide. The Muftis have been deployed and are scouring the chor bazaars and shadowing known antique dealers who do business with the Parsis. The drive of the operatives who are keeping the notes out of the hands of the authorities is commendable. Once out and into the hands of the technokings and oilroyals it will only serve to cement their control over their subjects.

3 responses to "The Notebook of Disquiet"

Speeder95, says:
April 12th 2027 9:17 p.m.

You're jumping the gun here by pinning this on the Arab monarchies, From where I am standing NATO has a greater vested interest in the Research (if there is any in the first place). The increased reliance of the west on the Indian subcontinent for its propaganda production rules out the govt. acting without oversight from the other members of the security council.

Narka XLR8, says:
April 13th 2027 2:34 a.m.

I am not ruling out interference from the west. But it is clear that the Immediate threat is to the Islamofascist states in Asia. It is in Uncle Sam's interest to not meddle and watch from the sidelines as this whole thing plays out. Any interference from the Yanks or the Limeys at this junction would only be to their detriment.

Ligmaz Bael Zhac, says:
April 13th 2027 3:17 a.m.

Historically that hasn't deterred them from getting involved. One of them will step into the muck to appease to the bloodthirst of their voters, and the rest will be dragged along like helpless fish through the complex networks of treaties and 'war' alliance mandates.

The space of the symbolic

The rise of CyberPunk Baba was proving to be a nuisance to Sri Sri Sri Brahspata. CyberPunk Baba was single-handedly undermining his hold on the University Students across the nation. His hold on the middle-aged middle class was unshakeable. However the inculcation of the freshmen by their immediate seniors was the core of his pyramid scheme. Cyber-Punk Baba's attack on Theology and Theosophy was winning over undergrads who in turn were disrupting the recruitment of new people into the Stylistics of Existing. Without them, he was no different from the hundreds of other Gurus who preached to the elderly on their decaying mats.

He wasn't the only one who was being affected by the endless tirade of rationalism. CyberPunk Baba was attacking all faiths. The usual strategies of siccing mobs of agitated Hindus or Christians or failing that issuing a Fatwa that worked wonders against Atheists were proving to be useless against the man. He had cleverly crouched his rationalism in spirituality. And his denunciations of the godmen were designed to be a call to a higher form of faith.

Any spiritual leader who was worth their salt would be attending the call today. He was counting on the support of HappyGuru, the Christian Televangelist Brother Gordon and the Islamic Televangelist Zulfikar Hashim to sway their fellow godmen. Every guru and cleric on the subcontinent who had a controlling interest in the youth would have reached the inevitable conclusion that he had; CyberPunk Baba had to be dealt with, and swiftly.

The space of the real

The penultimate issue with the Cinephiles for the Upliftment of Cinema and Kino Society was the infestation of letterboxd two follower essay types in its membership. The ultimate issue was the absence of women. One of the new members was in the process of tearing his storyboards. The older members were nodding in approval and some offered words of encouragement. A large group in the centre of the room was loudly debating the demerits of the duopoly of super franchises that had cornered the market, a few stragglers were scattered around the room, either scrolling through their feeds or reading pamphlets. He spotted Daris in the back and made his way to him. Vikram had severe disagreements with Daris over his misuse of Dutch angles but overall preferred his company over the others in the club. Daris softly nodded his head and passed him a copy of the pamphlet. It was a proposal to stop screening films that didn't pass the Bechdel test. Considering that the last time someone had made their proposal a la pamphlet was to start a dating app that was linked to letterboxd and imdb, it was a quantum leap, and would undoubtedly fail the community vote.

'Any progress?' he asked Daris hopefully.

'None.' Daris softly shook his head. 'There are players who are trying to incorporate noise and barcodes into their playing. But not in the way you've outlined.'

'And the prospective?' he mumbled.

'No acoustics. And most of what he was using were spliced up samples and freebies. Only changed enough to not get blocked or demonetised' Daris replied with an uneasy smile.

'Well then I am fucked' he sighed sinking into a nearby chair. The large group had broken off and people were looking for seats. One of the club heads was charting out the semester agenda on the whiteboard while another was setting up the projector.

Next to him, Daris began to drum his fingers on the table. Vikram could identify the timestamp, but not the tune.

'There is something.' Daris said turning towards him.

'Something?'

'Not a musician. But maybe a new project.'

Vikram shook his head, 'I need to stick with things. I keep throwing away projects.'

He felt Daris' eyes on his neck 'It could be something. It's set up for this weekend. I am in, but I don't really do documentaries or narrative footage. Tag along, maybe you will find your next project. Who knows, we might as well get a new lead on a Telecaster player.'

'I'm not saying no.' Vikram sighed. 'I don't know. I just keep looking for something that can really fracture things, you know. Really make a dent. But before I can complete it, something or the other falls through.'

'You're too hard on yourself man.'

'Haha, maybe.'

The projector flashed on suddenly and the words Cinephiles for the Upliftment of Cinema and Kino Society were thrown up on the wall in bright red. Vikram stared absently at the ceiling as gaudy ppt slides flashed on and on.

The space of the symbolic

Inside the hangars filled with endless aisles of cereals and jams and industrial strength cleaners, under the floodlights, hundreds of shoppers teem through the labyrinthine hypermarkets. They navigate the ant farm of produce and products looking for that hormone cocktail that hits the nervous system when you strike that perfect combination of savings, sequential irrelevant choice and last and the least the procurement of sustenance.

But there are others in the store who never make it to the cash counters. Petty Theft, Kleptomaniacs, Thrill Seeking Shoplifters? Not quite. These are respectable people who have fallen into hard times. Depending on the decade it could be the pandemic, the housing collapse, or whatever comes next. These are respectable people whose ritual Sunday shopping is something that is no longer a luxury they can afford. But the experience of shopping? That is still free. No laws against browsing and collecting things neatly in a cart if that cart is parked inside the store once you leave the premises.

The space of the virtual

Cortona: 23 year old found dead in his flat

In a suspected case of suicide, a 23-year-old was found dead in a flat in Cortona on Friday, the police reported. The deceased, Alessandro, was active on social media and was a member of various occultist websites.

According to the officer on duty, the neighbours had alerted them after noticing the rising pile of newspapers outside his door. The landlord told him that the youth was found dead in his flat when he used the master key to open and check on the deceased. The man was found dead at his desk and was officially pronounced by the attending at the local hospital. The flat itself was filled with images and books that one neighbour described as "deeply unsettling" and "unchristian."

Cortona police officials noted while prime facie the probe indicates suicide, a detailed investigation will ascertain the exact sequence of events leading to the death. The Officials said they would soon be recording statements from the family members of Alessandro and others connected to the case.

The space of the real

As he turned the page on the codex, Karna's eye fell on his untouched thermodynamics textbook and he felt a pang of guilt shoot through him. He had been drifting further and further into esoteric philosophy and theory, and his coursework was steadily piling up. He was suspended somewhere in the middle. The bottom was a dark abyss, the top lost in the clouds. Sometimes he wondered if he was climbing upside down. All he could do was climb, or stop and be stuck in Trishanku's heaven. The multiplicities were endless, and strange texts were exploding in the no-spaces.

'The food will be there in an hour.' his mother's voice travelled through cement, brick, and wood to reach him.

His new room was smaller than his last one. Things had changed but perhaps not as much as they had ought to. He had left the walls blank and all his posters were packed away on the top of the bookshelf. His eyes wandered to the dust on the shelf, he stood up and reached out with his finger. He could hear the faint noises of the weekly market being set up across the street. The setting sun threw up faint shadows across his ceiling. But with clear divisions of light and dark – the light changed for a moment as a car passed by his apartment building. A good half of his desk was covered with hyperstitional samizdats, theoretical tracts and schizoid tomes. The engineered wood was breaking through the veneer in places from the water damage. He rested his head on the desk and began typing on his Hermes 3000. He liked the way the keys felt against his fingertips. Although scarcely pressing down, so as to not punch a hole through the thin paper of the scroll that he had been working on for the last few weeks.

He felt his door creaking open gently.

'Akira?' he called out to his sister.

'The internet crashed' she poked her head inside his room. He could see the dark circles forming under her eyes.

'I don't think I should fix it. You could use some off time.'

'It's the final episode.'

'It's always the final episode.'

'Are you going to fix it or not?'

The Wi-Fi was getting buggier with every passing day. Not just the Wi-Fi, Karna corrected himself. There were a series of interruptions in K-Space. The flows were being disrupted and erupting more frequently. New factions formed and split within the course of a few days. Something was reorganising the virtual field. The movement was shifting. The pulse had changed.

But what was it changing to and who was guiding it? He had no answers. He could feel the uncertainty gripping the forums on the surface web. The coming hysteria was being actively celebrated in mad black cells of the dark net. Karna felt cautiously optimistic. But when he looked at the overarching hold of the techno-capital machine on the world around him, he wondered if there was any point in hoping for something else. He knew he would be better off if he buried the texts, put his head down and set his sights on a career.

The space of the virtual

Selections from the Leaked Transcripts of Committee Members President A, Education Minister B, Broadcast Minister C and CIL CEO D, Offices of Credence Industries Limited. Mumbai, Maharashtra; 15 APRIL 2014

C: This will never float. I know you think we can do anything, but I don't see how I will sell this. There is a limit to what the IT cell can do.

B: You're being short-sighted C. We need to stick with the same line of reasoning that has worked for us in the past.

C: Progressive Education Reform a la West is a solid formula B. But it must be present in the West in the first place.

A: If you have a better way to deal with the Student Unions then enlighten us C. B has done his job. Now you need to do yours.

B: There is a reason we have taken a leap forward in terms of quality; the application of what has already been carried out to its logical end. I am not sure the conditions for it exist right now.

A: The growing unrest in the councils is taking a disturbingly unified direction. And the opposition from the faculty and our youth organisations won't be able to keep up with the growing numbers. Fragmentation is the only way forward.

C: We will have to concede some amenities. Travel will need to be free, at least within the prescribed hours.

A: A minor hindrance to the taxpayer.

*

A: You're being uncharacteristically silent Mr. D.

D: As always, I am available at your discretion.

C: If B issues a statement about the need for the increase in digital education tomorrow, how long will you need to roll out your free internet program?

D: In the Metropolis? With the right permits, within the month. In Tier 2 cities, somewhere in the next three months. Tier 3 cities will take longer naturally.

A: We will expedite the paperwork. But Tier 3 is our major concern. We need to speed track the rollout of these reforms. B and C will you be able to put together a packet for dissemination in the given time frame?

C: We would need to pull in some think tanks, and you should expect overtime. A lot of it. But I don't see why not.

B: I'll coordinate with my counterparts. A goodwill push from them will go a long way in selling this.

*

A: C contact Banerjee and the other channels. I want this on Prime Time with follow-ups throughout the day.

D: I think there is room for aggressive expansion. I can see us rolling this out overseas. I hope I am not being too presumptuous.

A: Not at all Mr. D, this problem isn't endemic to our part of the world. We can begin the rollout through your subsidiaries in the subcontinent once the program is cemented here.

D: Mr. B, we can rope in Vasiraju's.

B: You won't mind splitting the Take?

D: I would have bought them out already if the founder wasn't still at the table. Regardless, the important thing isn't the Take. Their experience in translating EduTech to the subcontinent isn't something we can take lightly. The ruthlessness with which they manage to get the lower middle class to pay through the roof for their products when they can't afford two square meals is precisely what we need. They have permeated the middle class in a way we never will, the rollout needs their roster of celebrities.

A: I trust you will be able to bring Vasiraju into the mix.

D: Of course.

The space of the real

Pavan felt dizzy as he put the page down. He felt the coppery taste of blood in his mouth. Was this a death threat? He half-smiled.

He placed the letter and the envelope inside the thesaurus and closed it shut. He decided he could use some coffee. Pavan turned and looked at the clock. He hadn't eaten anything since he'd woken up. He got up, tucked the pages in his pocket and left the apartment.

The sun had softened now. He looked at the people as he crossed to the other side and entered the café. He placed his order and pulled out the page and some blank sheets he'd brought with him. He started working on separating the alphabets by copying them out on two separate pages.

Pavan had heard about this sort of thing once before. There were stories of a book written by a man called Herbert Quain. Statements. It was possible to draw out more than one story from any of the ten statements that Herbert had left behind. Many writers had wasted decades looking for new texts in the existing texts, only to find out someone had beaten them to the punch. There was a desperation involved in wanting to write and not being able to come up with things. He understood it well. More so than others. He had thought about looking for a copy, but that was next to impossible. He was a little-known writer from Europe, and his Statements had never been reprinted. Pavan was glad in a way that he could not access the book. There was no telling how much time he would have drowned in had he gotten his hands on a copy.

The condensation of the coffee had left a ring on the table, and now the water was slowly edging its way toward his work. This one page had taken up enough time to make his food go cold and the coffee warm. He shuddered to think what an entire book would do to him. He decided to speed up the process and started feeding the words into an online translation tool. Two stories started weaving their way into existence on the pages before him. He looked around at the empty café around him. The waitress was in the back now.

Evening had fallen around him. Some of the regulars had come in, and others had left. He checked his watch. It was a little after seven. The tables were empty and the soft orange overhead lamps had washed the room in amber. Lately, wherever he looked, all he could see was yet another piece of his life that had worn itself out irretrievably. Pavan did not enjoy coming up with new ways to keep himself occupied or entertained. Everything sooner or later took on the dullness of a routine. Nothing could survive his tendency to wear out to the last atom all that was once new.

He looked down at the pages. These were new. They were a break in his routine.

For now.

The space of the dream

The Librarian was an old man sitting on a creaky old chair that was balanced precariously on the mud under it. An ottoman lay overturned a little distance away from the chair. Tiny lizard like creatures were circling it suspiciously. He is lost in some book. The title is in a script that the man had never seen before. The book looks old and is on its last legs. Next to him is an almost empty bookshelf.

The librarian looked comfortable in his solitude. There was no one else on the island. There hadn't been anyone on the island for many years. He tried to catch the librarian's attention by waving his hand, but the librarian ignored him and went on reading. He wanted to pat him on the shoulder but he didn't dare. It somehow felt important to him, that the old man not be disturbed.

He sighed to himself and walked over to the ottoman. The creatures scampered off as he picked up the ottoman and sat down. For a few minutes, he persisted in turning over what he was seeing in his head, to solve the mystery but he was soon overcome with an indifference that was fuelled by the soft ocean wind on his face.

He looked at the land around him. It was a small island – small and round from what he could make of it. The slope of the land around him suggested that the place had been a volcano once. But it hadn't breathed fire in a long time.

Suddenly the man sat up, the arch of his back completely straight now. He got up and replaced the book on the shelf. The old man plunged his hand deep into his pocket and pulled out a pocket watch. He watched as the librarian adjusted the hands of the watch; pausing now and then, readjusting the hands.

Finally, the Librarian nodded to himself and began walking across the grassland. He followed him, at a distance. The librarian pulled out a compass and looked at it, changing directions subtly and unpredictably.

The volcano was silent under his feet. He felt the wind on his back as he followed the librarian to the western cliffs. They walked together for what felt like an eternity. The librarian took strong confident steps even when he changed directions. The man trailed behind him, looking at the blue ocean now and the vast expansive sky that stretched in all directions around him. Large tufts of clouds hovered in the distance. As they neared the cliffs, he could see the algae floating just under them. The ocean was eternally blue and singing as the water crashed against itself and the tiny islets at the bottom. He stood next to the librarian and turned his gaze in the same direction.

The sails of several little ships were visible on the horizon.

The portrait of his predecessor was an eyesore. He had become the Chief of the department almost a decade ago now, but the man continued to haunt him. It had to go. When he looked at D.O.M.A. and the heights he had brought it to, it felt deeply unfair to him that he should have to share the wall with the old coot. He would have had it thrown out long ago, but some loyalists were still in the department and he needed to keep up appearances. He was waiting for the man to croak. Back when Newton had taken over the Royal Society, he had done the same to Hooke. And when it came to the department, the Predecessor might as well have been Hooke. The Chief liked this parallel very much and would often find himself thinking about it.

The man's granddaughter was working for him. He saw a lot of himself in her. Young, ambitious, naïve, possessed of a certainty that allowed her to push forward with her work against the tenets of sheep morality. The Chief felt comfortable in letting her lead the research but he stayed close enough to the action to ensure that she couldn't do to him, what he had done to her grandfather. Navya had grown into a woman in front of his eyes. There were decades between the two of them, but he couldn't stop himself from sneaking a look at her every now and then. Later when he was sure everyone had left, he would summon up the image of her bottom, and the way the fabric curved around it whenever she was bent over the control panel. There had been moments when she had caught him staring, and the polite smiles she had shot her way had been the main reason he had never even considered suggesting anything of the sort. Fucking his granddaughter would be much more satisfying than burning a portrait, the Chief thought to himself as his eyes followed the mess of numbers on the budget report.

CardHoeSakura explains why she has "no sympathy" for Jaegerswaifu after breakdown

Sakura 'CardHoeSakura' Anys has taken aim at Grisha 'Jaegerswaifu' Bagchi after the Twitch streamer had a breakdown on stream. The Veteran Twitch megastar said that, while her situation is "horrible," she feels "no sympathy"

CardHoeSakura and Jaegerswaifu were at each other's throats last year, after Bagchi called CardHoeSakura a "Tired Old Twitch Thot."

The streamer asked if the new generation had any hope of making it big on the platform when "stretched out hoes pushing their late thirties" were still monopolising the platform. Bagchi went on to criticise the "Orientalist Ass Hoes who culturesteal for subs and clout."

Bagchi received a ton of criticism for the move among other things in her Twitch career — mostly her involvement in the major E-Lafdas that pervade Bong internet culture. Bagchi began to get threats from Sakura's fans after the latter asked her viewers to leave negative feedback under Bagchi's videos. Sakura's call to arms "Come on you Simps, Who will show mama that they're the real Pogchamp" has since been denounced by Sakura as an ill-advised move after it became the subject of criticism by her parent company.

CardHoeSakura claimed that while she is happy to leave the drama in the past, all she wants Jaegerswaifu to do is own up to her "sexist and ageist comments." The Streamer believes she has not apologized for some of the things she has done, and instead opted to shift blame.

Commenting on the harassment that Bagchi has been receiving from Anys' Simps "I don't feel sad for her. Play stupid games, Win stupid prizes. It is sad that she got depresso and what not, but to get my Simps to stop harassing her would be so easy. Just apologise." she stated.

- Read more: Grisha claims abuse of her cat on stream was an "accident"

Grisha has been the victim of Stalking, by what she claims is "One of the Incel Simp Orbiters that that Whore sicced on me." In September, the man spent days outside her house and managed to assault her before being detained by police. He was released with a warning. In November, the man began to send death threats to Grisha and her sister via her Twitch chat. Despite various attempts to seek help from her local police department, Grisha was told by authorities that there was not much they could do unless she is physically harmed.

While CardHoeSakura primarily talked about the incident between her and Jaegerswaifu, she also briefly mentioned more recent drama. This included when Bagchi threw her cat across the room for the 'Toss 'Em Challenge.' "It's Toss 'Em, Not Smash 'Em against the wall."

- Read more: Rumours surface: is BallsHog24 being investigated for Cocaine distribution?

She argued that the Twitch streamer "played into being a brown ass victim hoe," and because she refused to apologize, people became resentful towards her. Bagchi has raised concerns with the abuse that she has been getting and recently went into more details on one of her streams "You know that's how people die on the internet. There are these mentally unstable men, and they get drawn to women with platforms and voices, and eventually one of them is obsessed or deranged enough to kill the woman.

I grew up listening to these horror stories about how this would happen to women on 4chan and other shithole sites. I never thought this could happen to me on something as mainstream as this platform."

"Most of the Drama in her life is not even from our spat or feud or whatever you want to call it — she did the whole cat challenge, and leak shamed one of her own Orbiters into attempting suicide — and she didn't get banned. I think people's resentment was that she was just another person trying to climb to the top without putting in the work and she became the villain of the internet" Sakura added.

The space of the real

The order of things sometimes felt uncertain to Karna. Where did it begin? Where did it end? Humans are mainly temporal beings, Heidegger said that. But time isn't always as forward as he would like it to be. He could see his life laid out in front of him in discrete packets, taking place all at once, all together.

'It's your move,' he could see the dark circles under Zahir's eyes had grown.

'It is my move,' Karna moved his pawn to king's bishop 4. 'You've been getting any sleep?'

'An hour here and there. Can't seem to shake it off. Has been the same for the last few months.' Zahir's obsession with Caro-Kann was what always did him in.

'She's using you.' Karna moved without looking.

'I know.'

'And?'

'And nothing. I like being used.'

'Use your time for something better.'

'Better what? I'll probably end up being unable to move from my bed for weeks, and then just fall into plain old misery.'

'So, you're opting for Misery Deluxe instead?'

'Basically. Change is good.'

'Change is good.'

'Change is good.'

'There has been some chatter.'

'In Onionland?'

'Where else?'

'There's always chatter in Onionland'

'It feels different'

'Sure it's not the insomnia?'

'Being Paranoid has its uses. Near misses are better than being done in.'

'You looked into it?'

'I did.'

Zahir closed the app, ending the match halfway and put his phone inside his pocket.

'The papers are here. I can get you a copy. But you will have to go pick them up.'

'Are there more sets than one?'

'One would think. But I honestly can't say.'

'Be more vague.'

'Learn how to Tor and you wouldn't need me to describe things to you now would you.'

'I have better things to do with my time.'

'It's all cyber now, I don't understand why these things are moving about as papers in the first place.'

'The contents are sensitive.'

'Or Horseshit.'

'Or Horseshit. I can't know which until I study them for myself.'

'You can take down a small country in an afternoon with the right code. I don't see why you put so much stock in words.'

'We all have our own obsessions.'

'I would've been more comfortable if you were looking for parchas instead.' he handed Karna the slip with the address.

'Thanks'

'It was nothing.'

'It still might be.'

The space of the dream

The train was endless. Inside the unconnected compartments, the dying tried to avoid the stare of the dead. The train stopped once every day for five minutes. The dead were unloaded into lime pits and the living into the now empty compartments. They had dragged him out of his bed three nights ago now. He could feel his strength failing. They had given him no explanations. The whites of their eyes were the last thing he remembered. He buried his head between his knees and tried to rock himself to sleep for what he hoped would be the final time.

The space of the virtual

DoctorSax Today at 03:52
Why is the Cask all fucked up rn? @MonsieurNix @Rootlady

WarCriminal Today at 03:53
It's been crazy man. I've just been sitting back and enjoying the shit show

RootLady Today at 03:53
There's been a lot of drama between the Admins. I think they met

IRL and went out drinking

MonsieurNix Today at 03:54
Yeah. Sadmin couldn't handle Badmin. Badmin started speaking
in tongues and it was too much for Sadmin. He ran away from
the pub and was unreachable for the rest of that night.

WarCriminal Today at 03:57
Lmao, can't say it wasn't coming.

CyberPunk93 Today at 03:58
Heh, they've already split the group. And new ones are popping
up everywhere, Hard to keep track really.

DoctorSax Today at 03:58
Sounds sad af.

RootLady Today at 03:59
They're both creeps tbf

DoctorSax Today at 03:59
True. True.

MonsieurNix Today at 04:01
More and more of these groups are splitting up. Fragmenting
further and further. It has always been an endless series of bad
takes with them, so Its not really a big loss. This chat is a good
enough by product for me personally.

Doctor Sax Today at 04:01
Leftbook has also had a lot of infight splits recently. One of the
Fashie groups just had a coup.

WarCriminal Today at 04:03
insert confused butterfly man Is this an Accelerationism?

CyberPunk93 Today at 04:04
Behold a Man

RootLady Today at 04:04
Destruction is the only penance

Doctor Sax Today at 04:04
Not for such geese the dream of harmony

MonsieurNix Today at 04:05
Peepeepoooopoooooooooo

DoctorSax Today at 04:05
Closes Nomse and runs

RootLady Today at 04:09
Going back to sleep frens

CyberPunk Today at 04:11
Dark Deleuzians are at the gates and the lady yearns for her bed

DoctorSax Today at 04:13
Wake me up when it is Real Insurrectionist Hours and not before

MonsieurNix Today at 04:27
Night Night Gnomes

The space of the real

The first thing that Vikram noticed as he entered the room was the necks. A tower of crooked necks greeted him as he entered the musty sub-basement room of the museum. His hand instinctively reached for the hump on his neck and he felt his body loosen up. He would blend in seamlessly here, for all the wrong reasons. Vikram was unnaturally tall and as a result had acquired some unseemly postures and curves along his body in order to walk through doors without bumping his head against the frame, but more importantly to talk to the people around him at eye level. The people in this room, he knew had acquired their bent napes from years of looking at their smartphones. The rectangular room was right under the exhibit area. The chairs were all pointed toward the small podium in the right corner of the room, but none of them were aligned with the others. An ugly banner read 'MEMERS ANONYMOUS' in bright red IMPACT font on a cloudy white background. Daris was already in the process of attacking the refreshments table and was signalling to join him. The spread had to be one of the more depressing things Vikram had seen in his life. It reminded him of train food, but somehow drier and sadder. Daris was expertly assembling a small tray of carrot and cheese sandwiches with generic salted chips. Vikram opened the tap on the coffee thermos and waited as the cardboard brown mixture slowly trickled out into his paper cup. MA met once every other Sunday in three locations across Delhi. The chapters rotated venues and members could float in and out of chapters at their discretion. Although it was strictly advised to not do so for the program to be completely effective. The website had gone into the details of the Seven Step Program that helped people cope and eventually to let go of their Habit. He had taken a seat with Daris in the second last row and had a good view of the entire room.

The people were slowly beginning to settle in their seats. There was something truly unsettling in the faces of some of the members. There was an emptiness in their eyes, their movements sluggish. He wanted to talk to the girl in the row in front of him, but the way she blinked her eyes made him reconsider. He felt a sudden twang of guilt shoot through him. The voyeuristic nature of his and Daris' presence in the room, the eerie familiarity to a certain early 2000s Kino, the foul smell of the man sitting four chairs to his left, Vikram felt overwhelmed by it all. A man is standing behind the podium now. Vikram nervously adjusted his button camera, angling it towards the podium.

'That's the chapter lord,' Darius offered helpfully. Vikram raised his eyebrow in response.

'Think of it as the appropriation of faiths. Saturnalia to Christmas, Mannat the goddess to Mannat the prayer, that kinda thing. They're aiming to drop off the habits, but the lingo is still the same.'

'Sounds Counter-productive.' Vikram wondered if the man in the grey suit had ever admined a page.

Daris shrugged 'I think the ongoing justification is that it's easier to focus all of one's willpower on getting rid of one Habit at a time. They don't want to overload the already strained attendees.'

The speaker tapped on the mic with his index finger – a little too affectedly for Vikram's tastes. 'I'm happy to see new faces in the crowd. I hope the newcomers will benefit from the seven steps. And I hope that the old members will keep on benefitting.' The man then began to quickly outline the dynamics of the MA meetings and how the seven steps could Change Your Life and Improve Your Outlook. The man waxed on and on about the seven steps until you could see spittle flying out of his mouth. Finally at the end of his sales pitch, he opened the floor to the speakers. To his surprise the girl in front of him got up and started making her way to the podium.

'Hello I am Neha.' Neha went on to describe her years of struggling with the Habit, all of which was too morbid for Vikram. But he could see the people around him nodding thoughtfully to the pauses and cadences of her address. ". . . and the misunderstanding with the other admins only served to make the Habit worse. I ended up spending hours and hours simply researching new formats, old formats, fonts, and saturation. All of that to make sure the new page I started would be more popular than the one they had made. And even when I wasn't online, I would read and read and read everything from Etymology to Semantics, just to gain an edge over the other pages. And it worked for a while. I was the sole admin of a successful linguistics page and the only Indian in the whole circuit. I managed to diversify the content and even include Tamizh, Kannada and other Dravidian lingos in my content. I was going to spin it off into a group . . ." The more Vikram listened to her, the less sense she made. The story of her decline into the Habit had uncanny similarities to a lot of his own friends, and yet none of them had it as bad as her. For a stretch there Vikram had himself been the only Indian admin of a Kino group online so he could understand where she was coming from. The defining features were the same everywhere: initial ecstasy at being included in the inner circle that becomes gradually less fun, then significantly less fun because of the post-ironic saturation of the Eurocentrists and postmodernists, until eventually, you find yourself doomscrolling at three in the night, keeping CST or GMT hours just to keep up with the Content, which becomes gradually less and less actual fun and is now a physical need. A Habit now, instead of the former voluntary meming; then at some point suddenly just no fun at all but proper work, combined with terrible daily hand-trembling need for the smartphone, then dread, anxiety, irrational phobias, dim siren-like memories of fun, trouble with assorted authorities, knee-buckling headaches, mild seizures, paranoia about Content being stolen, painfully intricate watermarking of Content to ensure that everyone knows who the creator is, and a list of other maladaptive behaviours – then eventually making your way to New Sincerity and Wholesomeposting, and eventually tiring of that as well.

"After weeks staring at the business end of a door of the psych ward . . ." Vikram perked up. What was this chic on about? He turned to Daris who shot him a meaningful look.

The space of the virtual

XLR8

The Dialectical Rope-a-Dope
Thursday May 20th 2019
Categories: Pop, Boxing, Transcript

Ladies and Gentlemen a very good evening to you and welcome to the Zenith Hall in Toronto Ontario as we present the featured round of the evening brought to you by Ataraxia starring Bill Murray in Theatres March 15th, Dion5 the official beer of boxing, Tyrell Corp. the official sponsor of Dialectical Rope-a-Dope, '15 minutes to the perfect replicant.' This bout is sanctioned by the wbc the president Bartleby Mike along with the Ontario state athletic commission chairman Nicole Beepee the third Judges at ringside Meletus Brookman, Antyus Linetti and Lycon westfeld. All right fans, here we go with a bout you've all been waiting for: 12 rounds of boxing for the wbc and dialectical heavy weight championship of the world and now ladies and gentlemen in attendance and boxing fans joining us around the world live from the Zenith Hall in Toronto it's time for the main event of the evening *bell rings* Introducing to you first the wbc title holder in the yellow corner at 6ft 1in wearing black trunks proudly representing Edmonton Alberta Canada he weighed in at 219 pounds the Canadian free speech activist who is undefeated in his campaign in the professional ranks with a tremendous record of 34 wins no losses 2 draws with 27 big wins coming by knockout here is the acclaimed knockout artist the undefeated hard hitting reigning and defending wbc objectivist heavyweight champion of the world introducing the Red Lobster Dr. Gordon Stephenson!!!!!! And his battle ready distinguished opponent across the ring fighting out of the red corner standing at six feet nine inches wearing red trunks with gold trim hailing from Ljubljana Slovenia he weighed in at 257 pounds he is also undefeated in his campaign with a record of 27 wins no losses 1 draw with 20 wins coming by way of knock out ladies and gentlemen please welcome the unified world champion and the boxing sensation currently recognised as the reigning and defending dialectical heavy weight champion of the world introducing the Trash Panda Savoy Djinen! And we introduce our referee in charge Lenny Wayne.

Okay Gentlemen . . . now gentlemen we went over the rules in the dressing room again I want to caution you to keep this fight clean at all times protect yourself at all times and what I say you must obey good luck and touch them up all right.

bell rings Round 1

The challenger Gordon Stephenson Stephenson immediately surges out into the center of the ring and Stephenson is coming up more aggressive than Djinen in the first round with his close reading of the manifesto and is throwing out its conceptual errors left and right taking it on proposition by proposition. Good defence by Djinen and he's sitting in the pocket more trying to gain his comfortability he ate that right hand from Stephenson DJINEN COMING FORWARD AND DJINEN'S PRESSING THE ACTION by bringing in Lacanian Psychoanalysis to deconstruct duty and the by-productness of happiness and the foundations of ideology 70 SECONDS TO GO IN THE FIRST That was a shot My Goodness! There was a strong jab by Savoy Djinen that sent Gordon Stephenson back a little bit He's looking to use that extra brain that he's put onto give him that extra power that he felt he needed to put down Gordon in this fight Well Amy you pointed out that during the ring walk for Stephenson Djinin was throwing about his hands gesticulating and shadowboxing to keep himself loose while loudly sniffing Both men are in impeccable shape Oh good left hand by Savoy Djinen landed and a strong jab by Gordon Stephenson There's a jab A jab that snapped back the head of the Jungian.

bell rings

[Excellent first round by Savoy Djinen but Gordon Stephenson remaining calm]

bell rings Round 2

Savoy Djinen seems to be very comfortable in that ring Amy as Gordon Stephenson waiting looking for that big shot And it is round two as the Canadian is bobbing and weaving but the Slovenian's argumental jabs appear to problematic will he lay out the maple leaf in the second round What a fantastic moment would that be Amy but Gordon Stephenson has the highest knockout percentage in objectivist championship in history In his previous fight when he TKOed Katie Oldman with a AHA! GOTCHA moment but Djinen's jabs seem to be problematic right now for the Red Lobster There's a big jab it was a jab left hook kinda combination BIG RIGHT HAND that snaps back the head of Djinen That's Djinen tying up we're coming on 90 seconds to go here in the second round Both fighters exchanging big leather here Gordon looking to launch that deconstructive right hand that has put down so many idpol neoliberals Big right hand by Stephenson but Djinen dodges it well with his critique of idpol neolibs as capitalists *bell rings*

[Both fighters still at it even after the bell, and Lenny Wayne is separating them Beautiful fight so far clean punches ebbs and flows poetry blow by blow]

bell rings Round 3

Both men with very entertaining Stephenson is throwing a volley of light archetypical jabs with an allegorical dragon-sheep hook Djinen is eating it well Djinen moves in Push Stepping aggressively 'You define your enemy is the Post Modern Neo Marxists correct? Well let me ask you this' A RIGHT HAND that connects by Djinin He can be heard shouting now 'Where are the Marxists? Where are the Marxists? 'And a Dialectical Cross that Connects with Stephenson's abdomen 'Where are the Marxists?' An Overhand Right and Down goes Stephenson Down goes Stephenson Oh My Goodness! And it is only round three I can't believe what I am watching Anthony and we can see that the referee has begun the count and Stephenson is on the canvas looking up at the lights Wait Amy he's getting up Will he beat the count And he's up and he's up with fifteen seconds on the clock to go And Stephenson is moving in Can Savoy Djinen finish off Gordon Stephenson A Right Hand Stephenson is hurt Stephenson's legs are not underneath him He is in huge trouble no knockdown no knockdown

bell rings

[What an eventful round Amy it almost looked like the end for Stephenson but he is somehow still hanging in His legs are gone underneath him I know he is taking some heavy punishment from the Slovenian and looks utterly shell shocked in his corner now he looks fatigued His ear is bleeding that means the equilibrium is gone What a great observation Amy What a reversal we are seeing tonight Savoy is not leaving any room for error Stephenson is being outboxed on his own terrain outplayed at his own game]

bell rings Round 4

Blood streaming a little bit from the mouth of Stephenson Gordon Stephenson put down for what I believe is the first time in his career And here comes Savoy again Djinen looks tremendous here And down goes Stephenson again And he's still bleeding out of his ear Djinen lands a shot to the body right there Gordon Stephenson has to dig deep And another Right hand by Djinen Halfway mark in the fourth And look at Djinen go 'Give me some names go on who are these postmodern neo Marxists' 'The utterly impotent moralisation of the neolibs?' Stephenson unable to land a single shot Djinen needs to be careful when he leans in he's dropping that left hand it leaves a wide open Stephenson is bleeding from his mouth Djinen seems to be in control of the fight so far A right hand by Djinen Stephenson doesn't seem to be himself and it's probably because of the technical brilliance of Savoy Djinen

bell rings

[Let's take a look back Stephenson's not really landing that many punches Something is wrong with his legs but Savoy Djinen he looks exceptional]

bell rings Round 5

And they're ready to go even before the bell rings A Right Hand by Djinen He goes on the Attack! 'You mention Foucault, His main target was Marxism. . . the enjoyment of self-marginalisation' Djinen's swarming Stephenson 'Will you say to the people in North Korea Set our house in order' And that was a punch on the back of the head right there 'Why the choice between the personal and the political' Stephenson it feels is having difficulty with the physicality of Savoy Djinen 'Tea or Coffee Yes Please Personal or Political Yes Please' Djinen with a right to the body As a minute twenty has come off the clock in the fifth round The Lobsterman being pushed to the limit like he never has before in his career This is the fight of his life A right hand by Djinen Stephenson's having trouble with his balance he's held on to the rope for a few seconds blood streaming from the ear Anything can happen But this isn't how we were expecting the night to go Stephenson has his back against the wall He's looking for an opening but Djinen isn't giving him anything Djinen's got Stephenson against the ropes A barrage of punches from Savoy Djinen Unbelievable Upper Body Movement And now a combination Huge Punishment ITS OVER TKO

5 responses to "The Dialectical Rope-a-Dope"

SeeLobster17, says:
May 20th 2019 4:54 p.m.

I'm, I'm so disappointed by this. Professor Djinen absolutely tore apart all of GS's arguments and ligaments. Savoy Djinen just tore apart every part of Chaos and Order.

HattedGent, says:
May 20th 2019 5:16 p.m.

This will be the final time I will pay for anything Gordon Stephenson related, time to take a look at some of Djinen's works.

Fifthamendmentfan$, says:
May 20th 2019 4:54 p.m.

I'm actually liking this Djinen guy a lot, I thought he was going to be an SJW communist but he has a lot of good ideas and seems very genuine, Stephenson seems…. less sure of his ideas and I never thought I'd be saying that

BoredIntellectual88, says:
May 20th 2019 4:54 p.m.

Stephenson literally is shaking in his boots…It really feels like everyone subconsciously knows that Djinen is just schooling him in every way even Stephenson himself

Overlord1922, says:
May 20th 2019 4:54 p.m.

STEPHENSON G was seriously embarrassingly unprepared. People paid to watch this. GS was totally outclassed the entire time, regurgitating stuff I've heard in his lectures as a crutch the entire time. If anything good came out of this abject disappointment it's that I was introduced to Djinen

The space of the real

'When you work at a typewriter, there is a sense of immediacy to it.' Karna mused. Most people went retro to try and reclaim a part of themselves from the information matrix. As the omnipresence of the internet continued to grow there was an increase in the demand for analog tech. But what was the point of carving out time away from the grid when it has become an inseparable part of you? There is no time away from your consciousness or its contents. The time he spent on his typewriter felt like an escape. Perhaps it was only that; an escape from the world around him, an escape from the endless feed, from the endless fill in the sty of things and events. The pages were a ray of light to Karna. Hope at a formula for change. Nothing more, Nothing less. Buried under the mysticism, and the archaic ramblings. Something of use. Everything could be repurposed. Appropriated to an end that was more fitting to it.

'I just like the way film looks to be honest.' Vikram had his Bolex out again and was turning it around in his hands. 'Sometimes I think it's because of Mekas. He used to use an H16, and I just feel I have to as well.' He put it back inside his bag. 'Digital is definitely more convenient. Developing film is a son of a bitch. Not to mention finding reels is getting harder and more expensive every day.'

'Typewriters are pretty cheap if you know where to look for them.' Karna looked up to check the block they were in. 'As a matter of fact, if we keep walking this way, you'll find a repair store that sells them. Not cheap though. Any leads on your musician?'

'Not yet. I am starting to give up on it.' Vikram paused 'Might have a new project.'

'Trolling around for something or already found it?'

'There are meetings here, four blocks in that direction.' Karna looked to where he was pointing. 'In the basements, it's a weekly thing, PTSD-ish thing but because of memes.'

'A support group?'

'Of sorts.'

'Feels a bit extreme.'

'I think a lot of it isn't real. But this one girl, can't get her out of my mind.'

'Oho!'

'Not like that idiot. I think something actually happened to her, something other than what she's willing to share with the group.'

'All the same, it's nice that you're finally moving on. I consider this an absolute success.'

'Did you see Zahir out with his girlfriend?'

'Who hasn't?'

'I would much rather be alone than be stuck in the past.'

'Vikram, not moving forward is the same thing.'

'Speaking of which, how are things with your girl?'

'She's different. Good different. I'm surprised she's not actually bored with me.'

'Karna, as something of an authority on overthinking, my advice is don't.'

The space of the virtual

D.O.M.A. Medical Summary Report

NAME: XXXXXXXXXXXXX

IDENTIFICATION OF PATIENT: This is a XX-year-old female who was referred by herself. She was formerly a part of the XXXXXXXXXXXXXXX. She is a reasonably reliable historian.

CHIEF COMPLAINT: "I have a severe anxiety disorder. I have PTSD."

HISTORY OF PRESENT ILLNESS: At age XX, Ms. XXXXXXX had a nervous breakdown at her temp job and had to be removed from the premises by mental healthcare professionals. She was then recruited for the XXXXXXXXXX program. After exiting the XXXXXXXXX she referred herself to the therapy program.

CURRENT MEDICATIONS: XXXXXXXX 700 mg p.o. q.d.; XXXXXXXXX 200 mg p.o. q.d.; XXXXX 500 mg p.o. q.h.s.; Ativan p.r.n. dosage unknown. In the past, she has been on Prozac, Trika, and Zoloft.

PSYCHIATRIC HISTORY: She saw Dr. XXXXXXXX. She saw XXXXX. She is diagnosed with Post-Traumatic Stress Disorder, Depression, and Generalized Anxiety Disorder. She had counselling in Mumbai in 2019. She had inpatient treatment in Delhi in 2022 also. She has attempted suicide twice. When we tried to get her to talk about her attempts, she began to cry and would not speak of it anymore.

MEDICAL HISTORY: She has persistent migraines and is hyperactive. She has no history of head injury or MRI test of the brain.

No history of EEG, seizures, thyroid problems, or asthma. There are no drug allergies. She has no hypertension, no diabetes, no glaucoma.

FAMILY HISTORY: Significant for her father not being mentally competent. Her mother was depressed and was treated. Her mother is currently age XX. She was "an extreme alcoholic."

There is no family history of bipolar disorder, anxiety, nor attention deficit, Tourette's syndrome, or learning disabilities.

There is no family history of hypertension.

ABUSE HISTORY: None.

SUBSTANCE ABUSE: Significant for having used over the counter pills, but she stated she has not used them excessively. She has never used alcohol, tobacco, marijuana, or any other drugs.

HOBBIES/SPIRITUAL: She likes to listen to music and referred to something called Japanoise and Hanatarash.

LEGAL HISTORY: She has never been arrested.

MENTAL STATUS: The program has adversely accelerated her symptoms. She isn't cognizant of this fact and hasn't expressed any desire to pursue legal action against D.O.M.A. She has made her way to the sixth step and is eligible for sponsoring another former program subject. There are no long-term cognitive effects. The program needs to fine tune their method. (Refer to Navya's Department)

CLINICAL IMPRESSION: XXXX is a XX-year-old female with a family history of depression, mental incompetence, and alcoholism. She has not used drugs or alcohol, and she has been treated in the past. She has an extensive medical history and brought her medical records, and they were thoroughly reviewed. She also has not had good psychotherapeutic consultation.

Her existing symptoms although initially worsened due to her participation in the program are now more manageable. Seeing the impact of falling out of the programs on previous Vehicles, it is imperative that we get her to the seventh step. We will update the department as to the assignment period and parameters.

DIAGNOSES:

AXIS I. 309.81 Posttraumatic Stress Disorder. 296.53 Bipolar Disorder, most recent episode depressed. Rule out 300.81 somatization disorder.

AXIS II. Rule out 301.83 Borderline Personality Disorder.

AXIS III. History of XXXXXXXXXXXXXXXXXXXXXXXXXX XXXXXXX, migraine headaches.

AXIS IV. Psychosocial stressors: Moderate. She has no problems with the primary support group, she is currently speaking with her family. She has economic issues. She has problems related to the social environment. The conflicts between her parents are trickling down to her and both of them are attempting to manipulate her to their own ends.

AXIS V. GAF: 55, current. Highest in the last year: 63.

PROGNOSIS: Observation and Treatment. Although she is Docile, we need to observe if the replicate surfaces under duress.

TREATMENT PLAN: We discussed the diagnoses, Depression, Generalized Anxiety Disorder and Post Traumatic Stress Disorder. We also discussed the treatment; we discussed Hypnotherapy, as well as psychotherapy. We are starting XXXX 10 mg p.o. q.a.m. The rest of her meds will be replaced with placebos and the effects will be logged in for use by the R&D dept. The assigned surveillance needs to be upped to level 4 in order to ascertain the fluctuations. Need to assign three interns to log dream babble and search for mentions of the replicate or any possible references that can be connected to the same. Old records will be reviewed from when they become available, and she will return for follow up in approximately two weeks, which will be the middle of June.

The space of the symbolic

He watches her as she arranges the flowers. Her expert hand motions remind him of the way he curates his memories. Removing the thorns, and cutting off the excessive stem. Making what was into a pretty arrangement that will fade in a few days. A beautiful lie presented in the alcove of his being.

The space of the real

It was the smell that she couldn't stand. The smell of old people, of death. It pervaded the house. If she wasn't careful, it stuck to her clothes. A staleness that had become one with the walls. When their mother had died in the pandemic, there was no other place for them to go but to their Nana's. Now that she was working, she did not want to continue living here. But Torsha was adamant about staying, even if she had to do everything by herself. Navya really wanted to be away from the smell, but she couldn't leave her sister behind. The stuffiness of the bungalow was in stark contrast to the clean open air-conditioned freshness of the office. She kept to her room and used air freshener obsessively. Her window looked out into the street, and on some evenings, she would forget her surroundings. She hoped for rain more than anything. Petrichor would flood into her room. She didn't need the air spray on rainy days.

Navya was roused from her rumination by the sound of heels clicking up the stairs. She wondered what Torsha wanted. She had a feeling what it was and she really wasn't looking forward to it. The sound got closer and closer. Navya began to spray around more aggressively.

'He wants you to go to his study' She looked at Torsha. She was leaning on the doorframe dressed in a Navy midi and had her heels on.

'Going somewhere?' Navya asked putting the spray can back on the shelf.

'You could do with a night out.' Torsha crossed her arms. Navya felt a little sad when she compared her social life with her sister's.

'I could do with a night in. Going to stream that new show'

'The one with the gangsters?'

'No, the one where they time travel.'

'Oh, the one with that actor that died last year'

'No, No the one with the producer who turned out to be a molester'

'Aah, The one with all those airbrushed Milfs!'

'Yes, That one.'

'Really?' Torsha looked at her sceptically.

Navya shrugged. 'Well what else is there to watch?'

'Anyway, Binge all you want to later, he's getting restless'

'Mmmhmm' Navya nodded softly. 'I'll go in a bit. I really don't want to see his face right now'

'Be that as it may . . .'

'Navya' his voice rang out through the largely empty house.

'. . . he's old and you'll regret it later on.' Torsha finished.

'You'd think'

Torsha grabbed her and began to jokingly march her down the stairs to his room. They separated and she headed for her grandfather's room, while Torsha headed out. She entered his room. He silently gestured to the low-set cane chair next to his.

'How are things at the Department now?' he looked gravely at her.

'I'm happy with the progress.' Navya had had enough of this routine, every other day he would call her up and posture about in a way as though the Department still orbited around him and his policies.

'Good. Good. I don't approve of the research, but it's just as well.' This was the problem with all men as far as she could see. She had grown up in a colony filled with retired army officers. An impotent desire to exert complete control over the lives of others. Now that they couldn't exercise their will over their subordinates, then their women, children and failing that the children of others around them would have to do.

'We will be seeking an increase in our funding in the next quarter. The linguistics sub-department is planning to integrate NLP in their catalogue.'

'It's not something that I would advise.' No, you wouldn't, Navya thought to herself. That is why you're out. There is no point in being tied down by the biases and preferences of old men.

'I will convey your concerns to the Chief' Navya put on the faux serious face that was her go-to response to mansplaining.

'You do that.'

'Hmm'

'Bring me my dinner.'

'Yes.'

She got up and left his room, quietly closing the door behind her at an angle that he liked. The house felt incredibly dark and empty to her as she made her way to the kitchen to get his food.

The space of the symbolic

The memetic book of the dead

When you slice the layer cake of unremarkable things, what falls out? Who is pouring over the volumes in the Athenaeum of forgotten writers? Buried inside the memetic pool of the human conscious are the ideas that first found light by the banks of the Nile, at the shores of the Mediterranean, and on the banks of the Ganges; trickling down from their generation defining pedestals to everyday unthinking quintessential use. Every thought contains the germs of every thought that came before it.

How often have you looked at an elegant idea in a mathematical pamphlet from the 1700s or at a Philosophical proof from the century after that and thought to yourself 'Hey, I have already arrived at these conclusions independently' or 'Oh, I wish I was born a few hundred years ago, I have had all these ideas at a much earlier age than these Philosophers and Mathematicians.'

Are they your ideas? Or are they the ideas that were carried from the minds of the dead as a language virus and into yours across time and space? What thoughts would you have had if you were alive at the same time as them? What viruses would animate your movement, what thoughts would you lament then?

The space of the dream

The Athenaeum of Forgotten Writers

Someone once told me that the universe is an endless library. I can't remember who it was. I can't remember much of anything. Inside the small room that is the totality of all I can see, all that I can touch, hear, smell and feel. I sometimes struggle with the word 'endless'. The library I inhabit, had inhabited, will have had inhabited, and will inhabit is not endless. It is a single room with shelves on all four walls. There is no door. There are no windows. There is a chair here, and a table and a blanket. I do not remember how I came to be inside this room, but I know I came to it fully formed.

It is a strange sensation to be able to look at that chair and to know it is a chair but to not know who you are and why you are. The world of my room filled with these books, the table, the chair, the blanket and me are the limits of my understanding.

And like all individuals who inhabit library universes (finite or infinite), I spend my time reading. The books keep changing in their insides. Perhaps that is what endless is; Change. But they end or they stop being, so perhaps not. I read somewhere that the universe is an endless library.

How do you leave the universe?

The space of the real

In a blur of motion, two canvas shoes, a brown leather coat, navy blue jeans flew by him before collecting themselves into the familiar shape of a woman. His Ex was suddenly inside his apartment after who knows how many years. 'Your publisher gave me your address' Anamika declared, slowly turning to him as she eyed the general disorder of his domicile. Pavan was too startled by the intrusion to voice his indignation.

'I would have called ahead, but I didn't have your new phone number' she said. Pavan's eyes fell on the long streak of bright pink hair that peeked out from between the lush folds of her long black hair.

'Yeah, I don't give out my phone number.' he managed, staring at her absentmindedly. He saw her nose twitch and felt his ears go red. 'I'm sorry, what do you want?' Pavan moved to open the windows to help dissipate the stale dankness that pervaded the studio apartment.

'I have been receiving death threats.' she explained. 'For the last two weeks, creepy letters have been showing up in my mailbox. I thought they were harmless at first but the latest one contained a photograph of me on my way to work.' As Pavan glanced in her direction, a cold sensation crept over the nape of his neck.

'I'm sorry Anamika while I sympathise with your situation, I don't understand what you want me to do about it? Go lodge a complaint with the police.'

He saw a look of annoyance flash across her face. 'What do you think they said?'

'Yes, but why are you here?'

Anamika looked at him, silently weighing some thought inside her head. 'I don't want you to be mad at me. But I have been chasing leads on a story and I kinda used one of your names to apply for information. And I have been receiving mail under that name.' she finished.

He quietly walked over to his desk pulled out the envelope and handed it to her. Her face darkened as she read the letter.

'It arrived today,' Pavan said, attempting to conceal his irritation. However, he realized she was well aware, having witnessed so much of him.

'I'm sorry, I fucked up. It was just on a whim and now I've dragged you into this.'

'Anamika, what is this?'

'I'm still working on that part.' she had begun pacing around his apartment. 'Look I have to be somewhere right now, but I promise you I will fix this.' Pavan eyed her sceptically. 'Can you take a look at the letters? They are a cipher of sorts and I can't figure them out'

Pavan nodded. 'Give them to me, I'll take a look.'

'I don't have them here; I'll email them to you in the evening. I really have to go now' She turned around and walked out of the flat, leaving as suddenly as she had come in.

*

Pavan breathed out into the still coldness around him, blowing a stream of fog into the air. He had come across it so many times but never in those bits and pieces of his life that he liked to mark out as the 'real.' A part of him did not want anything to do with her but there was something about the frantic unthinkingness of her movements that made him want to believe her. He thought about her hair and the subtle hint of perfume that she had left behind in his apartment. He passed the old Regal as a river of people flowed in and out of the clubs. He liked walking around Connaught Place whenever he needed to clear his head. He turned at the end of the colonnade and cut to the middle circle in order to avoid the crowd.

Without any warning his nose suddenly caught the whiff of nicotine in the air, he looked at the small tobacconist inside one of the alleys and the two men nervously talking to each other, passing a single cigarette back and forth. He shrugged it off, quickening his pace. He didn't want to fall back into the habit. Pavan opened his phone, automatically switching and moving between the same three or four apps. He suddenly felt a pricking sensation in his thumb and felt the muscles tense up.

Whenever he was faced with any of the habits he had given up, he found his way back to the ones that were still here. He had given up alcohol, but now his piss smelled like coffee. It was not in his nature to give something up completely and leave the hole it left behind unfilled.

As he checked his emails, her name popped out at him from between all the spam. He opened it. She had attached all the letters she had received as attachments and asked him to update her if he found anything new. Pavan opened the attachments and scrolled through them, the page she had received and the translations were attached there. Along with the photo and the letters in pencil that had been scrawled over the paper. He could see the places where the nib had torn through.

Pavan swiped a little more, the Ouroboros again. Red. He swiped across it quickly to get to the last image. A rune started back at him. He had seen it before. Pavan quickly turned back towards the centre circle, dodging the increasing foot traffic and entered the underground market. The shouts of the hawkers quickly enveloped him as he made his way to the bookstore.

The shopkeeper threw out a half-hearted greeting as he entered the shop. Pavan moved through the racks scanning them as he went along and found his way to the book he was looking for: Eschatology and Symbolism in the works of Vorts Vijlandi. Three or four neglected copies were huddled up together on the bottom corner of the bookcase. He pulled out a copy and opened it to the right page.

The symbol was there; he ignored the text around it and tracked the citation number under the mark instead to the notes on the end. The author of the volume from which the symbol had been pulled was waiting there amongst the countless names. He yanked out his name from the list and typed in the author's name in the search engine. It spat out an uncountable number of research papers. He opened one and quickly shot him an email.

Now all had to do was wait.

KARNATAKA
Rationalist Cyberpunk Baba shot dead

M. Charvaka   Dharwad, August 30, 2027 12:31 IST

Three unidentified men arrived in a motorcycle at the residence of the self-styled Cyberpunk Baba in Dharwad and shot him.

In a shocking incident, Shantanu Karnad (47) — a Kannada writer and rationalist — who was known for his strong stand against superstitious practices and right-wing groups, was shot dead by two unidentified persons at his house at 10:20 a.m. on Friday.

According to his family members, Karnad was speaking on his cell phone when someone knocked on the door of his house. When he opened the door, Karnad was shot point-blank. The bullet pierced through his head.

His son said that after hearing the gunshots, they rushed to the door and saw Karnad lying on the ground. He was rushed to a private hospital, where he was declared Dead on Arrival.

Hubballi-Dharwad Commissioner of Police, Rajendra Sharma, said that a special team, headed by Commissioner of Police and comprising five inspectors, had been formed to investigate the case.

Meanwhile, sources in the police said that the role of fringe elements in his murder was being suspected. The manner in which he was murdered matches that of atheist leader, Krishna Patil.

The space of the real

The vast silent market in the Gunj where the men front as peddlers of amorantic injections and designer drugs while secretly dealing in antiquities, and dangerous texts and marginalia without the texts themselves.

Overhead cheap hotels with cheaper neon cast shadows of writhing bodies in brass beds cuffed or tied depending on the money paid, Firangis with tanned hides and broke accounts lying down in small rooms with backpacks and deathly calm wondering how long before nirvana hits and in open roofed hammock cafes scores of students slumming it up in the cool think tank areas of no-think and shoot-upload-eat calmness of dead eyes and places. Tibetan singing bowls lathed out in the door-locked factories of north Delhi, discarded film armour, mace, broken bows, and ketamine measuring scales and psychedelic print junk for the hipsters' interior deco jumbled in and repeating in the lined-up street side emporiums.

It wasn't his first time here. But the directions were leading him to an unfamiliar part of the market. He quickened his pace, moving deeper into the alleys that lead to old patchwork repair shops, halwais, homes, travel agencies offering packages for uncoordinated destinations, and dusty thin alleys with thin groove gutters on either side. This is the address. He looked at the half-closed metal shutter of the store. Karna could hear the footsteps inside the shop. Two hands came out from the dark and began to struggle against the rusty shutter. He resisted the urge to help. A mismatched pair of eyes looked out at him from the dark. The man turned on the lights inside and Karna was greeted by the bright and gaudy front of a bookstore advertising travelogues, porn, and novels in every language for the Firangs and Language students in the city.

'You're not afraid of a raid?' Karna asked the man, as he moved through the shelves. The stale smell of paper and rot in his nose.

'Like hiding a tree in a forest' the man replied without turning. 'You're welcome to browse while I get the pages.'

Karna turned around and looked at the piles of books, the ones on the bottom had practically melded together under the weight of the ones on the top. He could see the Nordic or Balkan titles in a box to his left while the more common French, Spanish and Japanese titles were stocked neatly and were alphabetised as well. On the top right corner, a series of glass cases boasted of Willy Shakes' First Folios, and fragments of Etruscan and Assyrian scrolls. The man had presently emerged from underneath his desk, climbing out from what could only be a hidden basement. He handed Karna the yellowed dossier. It was stamped with Arabic letters and on the bottom right corner had a green Ouroboros. He opened the flap on his satchel and carefully placed it inside.

'And the payment?' the man raised his eyebrows. The mixed colour of his eyes unsettled him for a moment.

Karna pulled out the cash and handed it to him. The man rifled through it with his thumb and looked satisfied.

'And now if you haven't found anything else to buy, I would prefer it if you left.'

The space of the virtual

Stand Up Meeting Notes from Vroom Call between Accelerationism Inc. guild leaders:

10 Jan 2026

- The L/Accs and the U/Accs have secured slots for image rehabilitation and improvement after the third school shooting incident this year by the Nazi/Accs
- The Stirnerites have rotated their week leader and will be represented by 5Argus in the meet
- The R/Accs have called for a vote against G/Accs to be held in the Bi-Quarter meet

New foundational opportunities in the Orient:

Textual Hyperstitions multiplying in Maghreb and the Deccan

Memetic Propaganda Outsourcing thriving under new management in India, Data Dumps by Anon suggest direct access to critical channels. Important to plant seeds in the Saffron Party Administration in case things change in the elections next year

- Possible mole points in Dept. Interniships
- Look into activating existing plants in Unis
- Consider Ether buyout of internal stakeholders in lynch pin positions

Stats for the Month:

Market penetration in NFT 9Chan at 77%, Quarterly target increments of 3%. Cask infiltration level Beta: One Admin and Two Mod IDs

Leftbook infiltration level Delta: 3 pages completely penetrated and appropriated, primed for accelerationism.

Rightbook infiltration level Alpha: 17 Groups, 3 Chatrooms, 14 Blogs penetrated, primed for accelerationism.

- The post-pandemic issue of Speederz is now open for submissions.
- Birthday alerts for Madmin, Jestmin, Brahmin. Crypto-Tokes and OnlyFans subs accepted as gifts.

The space of the real

The train lurched forward with a sudden jerk catching Pavan off guard. He looked up from his book. The light on his stop was blinking from across the other side. He slowly closed the paperback, making a mental note of the page number. He hadn't expected the Professor to respond as quickly as he had. The station announcements overhead echoed out into the empty platform around him. First in English, Then in Hindi. He stepped on the escalator and felt the wind from the departing train push on his back. He wondered how long it had been since he had taken the metro, perhaps in Year One of the pandemic, maybe not even then.

Pavan noticed the well-kept roads and the street plants as he came out of the subway. Old bungalows were lined up on both sides of the street. The buildings were dying a slow death. The Art Deco inspired façades were crumbling down. As he kept walking, he saw the garish new glass properties that had been built after tearing down the older structures. He couldn't decide what he hated more. He stopped at a large white house. The place felt like it was in the process of being turned into a hotel. He rang the doorbell and waited. A scratchy voice came from the intercom asking what he wanted. He turned to the camera.

'I'm here to see the Professor.' The gate clicked. He pushed it open and walked inside. The house looked bare, its empty hallways pronged out into three different directions. A man emerged next to him. 'Professor?' The man shook his head 'No. He's that way, I'll get you some water' and he disappeared as noiselessly as he had appeared.

Pavan found himself inside a study. Bookshelves rose and covered the room on all sides. The landing had its own bookcases and could only be reached through a narrow staircase in the centre of the wall in front of him. The professor was on the landing, frenetically flipping through various books. He would open one, change his mind, walk over to some other shelf take out a different volume, flip through it, change his mind again, rinse and repeat.

Pavan followed his movements with his eyes. The professor's Brownian motion between the texts was making his head dizzy. There was no use interrupting him Pavan decided. He crashed into the sofa and tried to not look at the man. The walls were covered in various maps.

'Who are you?' the man called out to him abruptly, his hands still curating, cataloguing the texts.

'I emailed you' Pavan managed.

The man nodded 'Yes, I remember. You're early. I am still looking for some of the materials.'

'Tell me what you want specifically.'

'The symbol in your book on Vijlandi, where did you get it from?'

The professor sighed 'There isn't much to know about it to be honest. Vijlandi got it from this cult that followed the Gospels of Tlön, the gospel itself is either a hoax or a pseudepigrapha designed to make people go in circles.

'In circles?' Pavan felt as if he had gotten a little closer to understanding the mental process of the man behind the letters. 'How do you mean?'

'Tlön isn't real. It was written by the Uqbari people, but the Uqbari themselves are a lost culture and there are no mentions of their city-state anywhere. And they're not lost in the way Akkad or Balanjar are lost but lost lost.' the Professor paused. 'There are maps of the city-state itself, and these are very detailed, but we don't know where Uqbar is.'

Pavan felt more lost after the explanation than he had before. He hadn't heard of any of these places and felt that the man was messing with him. 'Hold on, so is the map real or not?'

'As real as any lines drawn by men can be – It had a culture, it had a people, It had a language, and then it didn't have any of the three. There is not much evidence, and it is mentioned too sparsely in the extant texts that do survive. Needless to say, it is lost to us.

'How do people know about it then?' Pavan felt a sudden urge to retrieve his phone and fact-check the man's claims.

'Ah, you see. People don't. Well not really anyway. I am one of maybe five people in the world who do. When I found mention of this in some obscure magazine, I was too amazed by it and decided to write about it. The other four were kind enough to send me secondary sources. I paid to publish in some of the local journals, and voila I was an expert. Naturally, no one in academia batted an eye. No one in academia usually does.'

As the Professor went on, Pavan felt like he was in a confessional, and the man was more than happy to lay out the totality of his sins for him to see. 'The shoddy research aside, weren't you ever concerned that someone might follow up?'

'Oh, But naturally. The axe hangs over every happiness, but I covered my bases. I wrote to the other four about my need for some originals at least. And they complied. One of them sent a crate that arrived six months later, Covered in stamps from both sides of the Atlantic and then some. Most of it was reproduced by hand, so I didn't know what to make of it. A lot of it was just speculation about the culture and traditions of the Uqbari.'

'No look, how can you be sure that those are not forgeries themselves then? You said it yourself; they were reproduced by hand.' Pavan looked at the professor, hoping to see a change in his expression.

The man was nonplussed. 'Look here boy, this is nothing but some light-hearted Orientalism. Writing about places that they've never visited, about cities that run in perfect circles and people who speak without nouns and fire eaters and snake charmers, that is what the West did for centuries. How is the way they write about Uqbar any different from how they wrote about Delhi or Kolkata? I doubt the non-existence of the places they wrote about would have proved a barrier for any of them. I don't feel any guilt about engaging in a little harmless forgery, especially if it is limited to journals no one reads. That is their purpose. You bury papers in them, and then you can cite them as you wish.'

'I have something I want you to take a look at.' Pavan pulled out the page from his coat pocket and showed it to the man. There was nothing to be gained by arguing with him, he decided.

'Could this be from Tlon?'

'Tlön', the Professor corrected him. 'It is an encryption. The alphabet is used to code cyphers by some of the people who trade in this sort of knowledge.'

'But why?'

'They have a lot of time on their hands I suppose.' The Professor offered sensing his impatience.

'The box I received, Included a few of these from the last century. You're welcome to go examine them if you wish. They don't make much sense. Just unconnected pieces of text. I tried to find some string of narrative through them but I couldn't. Maybe you will succeed where I did not' He walked to the other end of the room and pulled out a book. He opened it and pulled out a folded page of writing from inside it. 'Here's the key.'

Pavan dusted off the chest and looked through the contents. The documents were there, and their translations. He couldn't recognise the languages. They looked European. 'Are these Uralic or Altaic in their root by any chance?' Pavan called out.

'Not quite. It's in Cimmerian or Cimbrian. I can never quite tell which.' The professor called out from the landing. 'They mutually wiped each other out in a civil war a few centuries ago.'

'Refer to these to read the scrolls' The Professor told him handing him old leather-bound volumes. 'It won't be very difficult, I have made notes in the dictionaries, you can refer to them.'

'Are you going somewhere?' Pavan asked as he watched the professor make for the door.

'There is a production of Pirandello at the University; I think I can still make the curtain call.'

'You can use my chambers, please don't touch any of the other books and ask the man who let you in to let you out.' Saying this, the man left.

Pavan sank into the large sofa and opened the first scroll.

The space of the symbolic

What ageless past lies between the Caspian and the Black Sea? What thoughts pass in his head who stands in the ruins of the shores of the Euphrates? I am standing in the river to tomorrow, a tedious rain on my face and tired feet that no longer want to struggle with the cascading water? The bacillus of doubt has hollowed out what little there was to begin with. The sloshing icy water freezing my ankles, the sweat of my fear ablaze on my skin.

What news of those who set out to walk with Giants?

They came back with heavy overflowing hearts and became insufferable talkers and annoyed everyone they met. Countless paragons of dead prose write on the ocean floor with their fingers. The simple act of playing a game of chess with a friend on a warm afternoon in a room with ample sunlight and a woman sitting close by looking half at you and half at her book can do wonders for the soul than any piece of literature ever could. Always in danger of coming into contact with long paperbacks with hammers for words that beat against the cranium endlessly and say only those things that we have always known.

The space of the real

Anamika's office was in the middle circle. But the entry was inside one of the alleys that cut in between the circles. The staircase that led up to the first floor was broken and somewhat mossy. The outside of the buildings got a new paint job annually, but the insides were always in a comical state of disrepair.

'Alright you've got me here Nirava. Who is dying?' she called out to her boss across the bullpen.

He put his tea down and gave her a disapproving look 'You do know that I cut your cheques.'

'You fancied an afternoon chat?'

'Nyra has been working the D.O.M.A. leads. We feel that there are more players involved.' Nirava scratched his chin. 'From what we can make of it, there are other parties interested in whatever it is that they are cooking up in that nut house.'

'Any idea who exactly?'

'None at all but these people are clearly unhinged enough to threaten us and hinder our work just to keep us from getting to what D.O.M.A. has in the works. Nyra will chase, So will Aruni. We will find out something soon.'

'Yeah, I've been doing some chasing of my own.'

'Care to share with the group?'

'If it gets somewhere, then yes.'

'You know Anamika, No one here will blame you if you took it a little slow after what happened.'

'It's ancient history now.'

'Three months isn't ancient. It's bad enough you're not taking counselling or talking to anyone about this. But keeping us out of the loop is idiocy. It's like you're looking for something bad to happen again.'

'Calm down boss. I will bring you in as soon as there is something. I'm not looking to get my picture on the wall that badly.'

The space of the dream

The Librarian of Kowloon Walled City

Has the night always been this loud? How long before it goes quiet again? The sparrows are sleeping in the bougainvillaea bushes that cover the barbed wires and metal spike fencing. There are sounds out there that he has never heard mixed in with the cries of grasshoppers and the howl of the dogs.

The building is condemned. What a strange way to put something so simple. It almost makes the building sound alive. Complete with a Fate and everything; beyond salvation. But there was some truth in it. The high-rise was unsalvageable. The last few months had been hell. The racket made in the name of seismic retrofitting had driven most of them out of their heads. It was almost a mercy that it was done and over with. The apartments were no good, and had to be taken down.

*

Once there was a city and then it wasn't. That is the story, the rest is history.

Inside the walls of Kowloon, the old librarian sits waiting. The clicks of his Olivetti bounce against the walls of his tiny room. The shelves on his walls are buckling under the weight of the volumes. Silverfish and mould have taken over some of the books. The ring of the typewriter's bell rings out, he slides the carriage back into place and continues feeding in the numbers.

There isn't much work for him inside the walls. And he enjoyed bookkeeping. It helped him take his mind off other things. He looked at the volumes of Burroughs and Miller mixed in with single-order pornos. He had to send out a copy of Bataille, he reminded himself. Or was it De Sade?

The whorehouse was not that far from his room. What was taking her so long? He pulled out his pipe and lit it. He pulled in deeply on it, holding the match to the tobacco, and released the smoke without inhaling it.

The fumes spiralled out and dissipated before reaching the ceiling. Soon enough the whole place was filled in with a thick haze that blurred out the names and titles of the books around him. Or perhaps it was just his bad eyesight, He smiled to himself.

There was an uncertain knock on his door. He invited her to come in. His tone was soft but commanding, leaving no uncertainty about the nature of their transaction.

She entered the room, taking small timid steps. She had a plain face that was caked in make-up. He had no doubt it had been the proprietress's doing. The smoke circled and moved around her, lending her a supernatural aura. He wondered if she would melt down at his touch. As she moved in a little closer at his invitation, he could see that he had done her a disservice. Underneath the mascara, her eyes were steeped in a cold rage.

It had been a decade since that day. The city council had razed down the City of Darkness. He was walking around with his cane in the park that stood where the city once had. As he rested on his cane and watched the remnants of the south gate, he could still remember her eyes.

*

The man was on his balcony now.

He felt the bitter taste of coffee rising in his throat. He gritted his teeth and swallowed it.

His friends were asleep on the sofas inside. They had helped him pack up the place. One of them had even invited him to stay with her until he figured something out. A half-played game of chess was spread out on the carpet.

They weren't going to demolish the building. They were going to deconstruct it. The windows and the doors from the empty apartments had already been stripped down. When he left tomorrow, the same would happen with his place. In a few weeks, they would begin with the roof, and then work their way back down to the faulty foundation. The bricks would be separated from each other and sent out to wholesalers again.

The balcony he was on was ugly. There was no other word for it. It belonged on an old brutalist building somewhere in the Eastern Bloc. Perhaps it was for the best that it was being taken down. The railing wasn't even aluminium; the builders had installed mild steel and painted it silver. The paint had already come off in several places.

Everything had a shelf life. This building had expired sooner than anyone expected, that's all. The land would be empty once again, and patiently wait for another building to rise up on it and fold the landscape into different shapes. Or perhaps it would all end up in a parking lot. His thoughts flitted now from the dying old people in the Danchis to the balconies of trash in old Panelhaz, to Favelas in the tropics and back to the slums that dotted his city.

There is something ineffably beautiful in the death of a city. One day it is. And then next it isn't. Pompeii, Hiroshima, Nagasaki, Epecuén, Pripyat, Vijayanagar. Compared to them this was a little death. And even then, they didn't remain dead, some of them came back.

Cities are never finished.

*

How much of our time is simply spent in dividing up space into more manageable units. Sizing up and weighing expanses and volumes into rooms and halls. How much of our time is simply spent in dividing up time into more manageable units. Sizing up and weighing events into days and weeks. Splitting up narratives into years and seasons and sometimes into the weathering of bricks under the rain.

The space of the real

The text was fractured. Displaced in time and space. It was schizoid. The rhizomatic nature of the connections made his head hurt. It was painfully obvious that these were in some part constructed or crafted for the explicit purposes of advancing false scholarship. It wasn't perhaps as bad as some of the other Apocrypha he had come across, the endless list of Grimoires which were appended with incense rituals with the business information of the incense seller who had undertaken the appending, Jatakas and Pachisis modified with certain jewels or tantras to boost the sales of the kitsch that was easily available but not in demand, astrolabes and aether detectors advertised on the fringes of sigillum deis – he couldn't see what purpose these texts served without a con affixed to them.

Karna half considered uploading some of the writings on the Alchemical forums online, but decided against it when he realised that they were more likely to read things into the texts than they were to find anything that would help him immediately. He might as well dump it on the conspiracy theory boards.

The ultra-macabre carelessly splashed over paper, the intensity of someone writing their heart out in blood. The consistency of a finely chopped word paste that dizzied the senses and confused the mind. A microcosm of instability. Waiting for its layers to be peeled off. And underneath it theory or perhaps poetry. If there ever was a difference between the two.

What he wanted above all things was not the solution. But a part of the puzzle that would fit in with the others he had collected or worked out himself. He would stitch them together. There were never any major breakthroughs. Every little thing had to be fought for. Every step forward was riddled with contradictions that had to be unknotted, every gash needed quilting. The sheet handed out to him was the same as everyone else. The way he folded it would make things, or break them.

The space of the virtual

Vikram's first and last letterboxd review written on ट्रेन रहति प्लेटफार्म (transl. Platform with no train) directed by Debi Dhara released in 1971 after its negatives were found in the director's belongings during the reading out of his last will and testament
  – 3 people found this review helpful.

Why do people constantly ignore the fringes of parallel cinema in this country. . . Sometimes I wonder if there is any capacity in the film watching youth to engage with more than three or four big Bengali names of the 70s and 80s. The surreal cinema of Debi Dhara is a joy to behold. A critique of the savarna supremacists par excellence, while being deeply humanistic. Almost approaching something like Anti-Cinema. The life and times of Debi Dhara are captured on celluloid in his Docu-Poetry Films about the Bengal Famine and the loss of identity in the face of the Bhadralok occupied with its own wittiness. The cinema of Debi Dhara is a testament to the human spirit. This is his only work in Hindi. In Platform with no train the doctrines of Manu reach Derridean hauntological heights never seen on film before. The materialism of Varamhira sharply cuts the fabric of the trainless platform as Dalits and Savarnas wait for a train that will never arrive. This Beckettian sense of waiting, is further heightened by the refusal of either group to speak with the other. The homeless drunk who breaks the silence in the end by asking 'इस्की माँ का चोदा ट्रेन कहाँ है बेहेनचोद' is perhaps the only one who manages to be Outside the always-already that animates the characters. The cinematography is kept at a minimum, but perhaps rightfully so. With this piece Debi certainly deserves to be considered on equal footing with Buñuel or Ozu. Sometimes I wonder how many more gems are buried or lost to time.

This was it. She was it. He zoomed in on her face, the pixels exploded and he looked at the grainy outline. It had been two hours since he'd sat down to edit. He played through the spliced assemblage of clips. There wasn't any audio. It had been some months since he had felt himself this immersed. She'd made an impression. He needed more footage. She hadn't been honest during her talk. So there was definitely a story there. Something semi-docu maybe with word-cards layered in with commentary. It could work as a silent. Not black and white. But grainy, yes. Cuts, Angles. He'd need to put in a lot of hours to make it work. It needed a longer runtime. Not feature. Darius was a bloodhound when it came to chasing subjects. Over the last few years, he had made himself indispensable to the circuit. Zooms always reminded him of censorship. The way the violence was cut out from international films, or the erratic zooms of illegal uploaders on YT trying their best to escape the algorithm.

Neha. Earthly tones. The music. Again, a roadblock. Maybe something simpler. Hopefully, the situation with the previous piece will get sorted by then. Vikram penned down the equipment that would best suit the situation. The aspect ratio had to change, between the guerrilla footage and the formal interviews. A dizzying opening montage of half words with absurdist frame inserts. Something that had a story to tell but wasn't too bogged down by narrative or characters or time or sense. Something fluid but discrete. He had to get the submission deadlines of the film fests this year. An Anti-Documentary. Something new. Maybe with a pinch of Mekas. He looked at the undeveloped film stock lying on the shelves. This had to be a complete thing. He had to finish this.

His eyes split her apart into the difference of her parts. Her eyes did the same to him. She wasn't her to him. There was just a torso there, with her breasts cupped up in her front latch bra. She blocked out his face. He wasn't him. He was a blank, and not one to be filled. But to be left as is. When she moved on top of him, he forced his eyes to not move above her neck. The muscles in her abdomen were tensing and relaxing. She placed her left hand on his chest. He was a blank. Just something to move against. To push against for a little while. He wasn't a fantasy or someone from her past. He wasn't the result of some unresolved anxiety. He wasn't.

As they shifted positions, for a moment the threat of her becoming something more than a torso loomed on the edge of his mind. Her legs brushed against his. The nerves in her hand stood out as she put her weight on them. But they vanished as soon as they reached a new equilibrium. He wasn't even a blank to her now. She couldn't see anything. She could feel him moving against her, through her but he was no longer a person. Almost a Thing. A thing to struggle against. A thing to feel inside yourself at the end of a long week. A stray thought that comes out of nowhere and goes nowhere.

Her head was buried in the sheet now. He felt the curve of her ass in his hands. She was a nice ass. They both came together, the faceless man and the headless woman, and as they pulled apart and hit the bed both of them felt a small sense of something that was achieved and on a deeper level a dissatisfaction that neither could put into words.

The money had been flowing in as promised. All that was expected of him in return were updates on the mimesis project. He didn't really see it as a betrayal of the Department or his own values. He knew that the project wasn't really headed anywhere. Navya was delusional. Seeing promise where there wasn't any. The Chief didn't really mind that though. The discards helped out with the menial chores around the department, and their families were happy to be rid of them. The Cylinder inspired awe in the auditors and visiting dignitaries and was enough for him to ask for the necessary raises in the budget that he needed.

He had been keeping a close eye on the progress of the project, but the real money came in from the Memetic Spin department. He had to give his predecessor credit where it was due. The shrewdness of a man who had created an entirely new job profile for the unemployed louts when he himself had no grasp of the technology involved was a force to be reckoned with. He had learned first-hand how to keep the orbits of the bureaucracy and those of the talent from colliding with each other. He hated to admit it but at times he felt acutely aware of his own age and his declining prowess with the accelerating technology. The money came in, the information went out. But he had put his trust in the invisible third party to keep him covered. He could have contracted the work to someone else, but he had learned early on that two men could only keep a secret between them if one was dead.

And it wasn't like the research itself was completely invaluable. Things have the value that other people believe them to have. And the successes of the Spin department put him in the unique position of being able to leverage the information for a comfortable retirement on a nice island nation with no extradition treaties in place. The payout he had been receiving right now was a drop in the ocean, but he knew it was better to be safe than sorry. And what little he was really leaking would be of little or no use to anyone without the full parameters and the design details. His mistress had been after his life for the last year to leave his wife and settle down with her. But he had no such plans. He wasn't going to carry any deadweight when the day finally came.

The space of the symbolic

The Abhuman body is one that mutates and becomes-other-than what it was. The self-determinatory and self-revisionary instincts are activated in response to radical change in the physis. The tipping point that is reached after slow accumulation of anomic aggregates within the body leads to the becoming-other-than of the Abhuman. The becoming is tied with a monstrous hubris that asserts its will on the materialities around it. The Abhuman may also be understood as the becoming-asura of a sentience that has long been relegated to the status of the living dead by the necropower of the state. The Abhuman body finds its instantiation in the ten headed asura Ravana – a sentient who rid himself of all the governing illusions of the self except for the 'intellect.' The Abhuman is intelligible to themselves, and to other becoming-other-than what they were. The Abhuman resists totemisation and symbolic reduction. The Abhuman body is an assemblage that is disassembled and reassembled based on the needs of the self-determinative needs of the Abhuman. Abhumanist cartography is not concerned with terra firma but with the intervention in and liberation of other Abhumanist bodies and becoming-other-than what they were. The Abhuman navigates and tests new horizons for their own expansion.

Excerpts from Pavan's Blog 'Before Dawn' created and last updated on 17th January 2019

9

He saw her for the first time at fall's end. She was dressed in a pink t-shirt, which he later found out was technically a coral top. She was reading Grapes of Wrath right across from him in the metro. He was listening to some metal band or the other, and it was practically consensual ear rape at this point. But he preferred it to overhearing the bigots and floozies on the blue line. She was wearing earmuffs over her earphones, so they really looked like headphones. She looked a bit silly, but with overtones of adorable. It was the intended effect.

11

The next time he saw her, it was on his friend's timeline. It was a photo of them in some café celebrating the end of exam blues. It was hard to recognise any of them because of the pouts they were sporting. But she was wearing the same top.

A quick conversation with his friend revealed that her name was Anamika and she was indeed single. In the following days, after assuring his friend that he would tone down on the intensity and be a perfect gentleman to her, he finally got her number. They met each other at friend A's New Year's Eve party that was actually held two days before the event it was set out to celebrate. Everyone had plans for the actual day, and no one really wanted to waste the New Year getting drunk with their friends.

There were bad days, and then there were really bad nights. The mornings following the good nights found the pair on the balcony of his apartment. The view was fairly pedestrian. But the third-floor apartment ensured a privacy that is extremely treasured by young adults living in a society of nosy gossip mongers. The wide berth given to them by the residents shrunk by a sizeable amount in the off season of the reality shows.

He prepared coffee for the pair of them. In the absence of any good coffee shops in the vicinity, the pair settled for instant coffee that was often over brewed. He sat on the balcony chair and started on whatever obscure work of fiction he was reading that week. She came out with her headphones, having added copious amounts of milk and sugar to the otherwise bitter concoction that he preferred.

They never talked during the ritual. She sipped her cloyingly sweet coffee and proceeded to make out with her cup. She slid her lips gently on the ceramic, letting the dark liquid sit on her lips for a while. Then after drawing unnecessarily long breaths, she'd finally take in a small sip. A tug at her shirt here, hiking her running shorts up to the point of discomfort.

It was for his benefit that she engaged in this ungodly objectophiliac fantasy. His darting glances were a source of unending amusement to her. After a while she started grooving to the songs, ever so slightly at first. Making it more pronounced as time passed by.

And when he couldn't take it anymore, he snatched the cup out of her hands, ripped off her shorts, leaving the headphones on. And they fucked again. She left in a hurry after that. And his little two by two was quiet again.

Living in a state of perpetual joblessness, he whiled away the day carefully curating the memories of the last one. The scent of her hair was still fresh on his pillow, and of her sex, on his sheets.

He read in this intoxicating environ for an hour or two. Sometimes he wrote poetry. She suffered in his poems, as every muse does. He crudely sculpted words around her absence, trying at once to capture some insight from the backwaters of his mind.

After he had gone through the act of assaulting paper with his hideous poetry, he went on to fix himself an early lunch. The hours following that were sacrificed at the altar of either the latest TV show in vogue or to some allegedly underrated Avant Garde technicolour.

He did not work on the really good days.

The space of the real

His office was dour. He had tried to give it some life with some abstract expressionist paintings. Motel art equivalents of Pollock and Sobel were housed in little alcoves lit by soft yellow lighting. He had paid for the remodelling himself once her grandfather had retired. Despite the excessive remodels, the smell of decaying paper filled the room. The stench of the rotting books mixed in with those of the varnish from the new bookcase he had gotten installed over the weekend. She felt trapped between the two men. She had a deep dislike for both of them. It wasn't a given that the position would be hers if the Chief died, but Navya knew she would be in the running. And it wouldn't be hard to pull in some loyalists. Maybe a deep clean or perhaps something that was more thorough. He enjoyed making people wait. It was his way of feeling important. She checked her watch, unlatching it and then latching it back on again. He had gotten rid of a lot of things, but he'd kept the desk. It was African Blackwood. Her grandfather had gotten it from department money and had to leave it behind when he retired. She reached out and felt around the underside of the overhang. She stopped as her finger brushed against the engraving. It had been twelve years since she'd made it, with her compass. Her grandfather's initials, hers, her sister's and her mother's were all there together inside a little heart 'N – T – M - T' ; Simpler times.

Things were scattered around the desk. Personnel reports were piled in a corner, Weekly stats in another. She picked up one of the ugly green folders and opened it and scoffed when she saw that the contents had been redacted. Typical. She moved everything back to its place and went back to the couch. Her feed consisted only of the news, and groups. Last year she had unfollowed most of her friends. All her friends were either getting married or were on their second kid. The wine mom jokes just got on her nerves now. Maybe don't flush your career down the drain and then cope about it on the internet.

'Thank you for waiting' she looked up from her phone. He had walked in noiselessly. Creepy bastard.

'Not an issue.' she watched him slowly make his way to his sealed window.

'I sincerely wish they would open.' he sighed.

'Can't have the Vehicles jumping out.'

'What of the EOS reports?'

'Stats are looking good. Trying to up the replicators per cycle but we seem to have hit a plateau.'

'Hmmm.'

'We'll get there.'

'We'd better. It won't be my neck on the line. You're the lead researcher.'

Navya threw out one of her practiced smiles at him. 'How is the memetic lit. department going, sir'

'Very nicely. The Balkans and the Steppes have been a great cultural addition. The language learning is slow. But the governments are happy with the cultural retooling kits.'

Black propaganda. Navya thought to herself. There was a lot that disgusted her about the department. She was willing to overlook a lot of it. Her research took precedence. Her work would redefine the ages to come. And she had no issues being in bed with D.O.M.A. to get there. 'That is excellent news'

'Just so. We are in negotiations with South Ossetia and Abkhazia. The Tibetans continue to badger, but not worth jeopardising our bilateral relations with our counterparts in Shanghai.'

'Have the Eritreans signed on?'

'Not yet. But I see it is on the horizon. I see great things in the future Navya. Deliver on this project and you will have a more secure hold on the department when I retire. Unlike the flaming mess I received from your grandfather.'

'Yes Chief.' she bit down on her tongue.

The space of the dream

The Ice cream vendor twirled the long-handled paddle and dipped it into the Barrel. He could see the yellow in his eyes. He winked at him – gave his heavily waxed moustache a twirl and went back to churning the barrel.

Atam looked down at the cone in his hand. Soon the ottoman dressed in the yelek vest would put the sticky Maraş ice cream in the emptiness. Atam raised his other hand and rubbed his eyes – for an instant he felt that someone was calling out his name.

The vendor smiled ear to ear and put a scoop in his cone. Atam looked down in horror. It was a mesh of human body parts that were still moving.

'Atam!'

His grandfather stared out in despair from the mesh. Before he could even understand what was happening – the vendor took the scoop away from him with the paddle.

Atam crushed the cone in anger. Without missing a beat, the vendor put another in his hand, and put the scoop of living corpses back in his cone. Atam reached out for his grandfather's tiny hand – the vendor pulled at his paddle again and he was again left with an empty cone.

The man had handed him two cones and pulled out one of them.

The ottoman winked again and crushed the cone. He tried to speak but he had no voice. Somehow all his words had been taken away from him.

He returned the scoop to the barrel and with a twist pulled out the entirety of the contents.

A large dome like mess of blood, bones and muscles was floating in the air tethered to his paddle – Atam looks at the dead faces crying out in agony. He couldn't see his grandfather in the jumble of the dead. The Turk placed them on his cone and then playfully returned them to a different barrel. Lost to time.

The space of the virtual

Abstract of Karna's First Year Research paper proposal rejected by the University's Philosophy Department

Paper Title

The Myth of Trishanku: Complex Identity and the Ethics of Living a Moral Life

Paper's Abstract (1600 characters max)

In a nutshell, the paper presents the issues of identity and the ethics of living (a good life) through the lens of the Indian Myth of Trishanku, as the man who is eternally suspended upside down between Heaven and Earth as his punishment for attempting to enter heaven with his physical body. Trishanku dwells in a private 'Heaven,' turned upside down and is used as a cautionary tale against postmodern, post-structural and/or complex tendencies in issues of identity and ethics. I will attempt to redefine the myth by turning it on its head, not unlike Trishanku himself.

The displacement of the King Satyavrata to the position of

a Chandala under the new identity of Trishanku after his questioning of the persisting dualism of the time, and his attempts to be a materialist who wanted to ascend to heaven are also explored through the lens of caste.

Heidegger's Mitsein and Dasien, Levinas' Other, Nietzsche's dichotomy of Apollo and Dionysus, Camus' Myth of Sisyphus along with Derrida's work on humanism and ethics is used to understand the Complex and Post-Structural nature of Identity and the ethics of living. Ambedkar and Periyar are used to explore the cost of rebelling against Manu's Idealism and the position of Materialists like Bhramagupta and Varahamira.

The identity established hitherto is explored through the Mythical Trishanku, and his eponymous Heaven. An attempt is then made to establish ethical praxis by using the identity of Trishanku as the grounds for an ethical life with emphasis on Otherness, Being-with, and Being-in-the-world.

The space of the real

Chi sat behind the wheel of his sedan. Leaning back in the plush leather. The back exit of the office building he was watching was washed in the flickering glow of the streetlight across the street. Chi was waiting. Chi was looking forward to tonight. Nothing unrefined today. Just the way he liked it. No point blanks, No silencers, No Metal. He breathed out into the car. He always had a small one stashed on the underside of his passenger seat for emergencies. Nothing but Catgut today. Clean. No fuss, No muss. Personal. Pure. Heavenly.

You know how people say, do what you are passionate about

and you won't work a day in your life. Not true. A lot of his clients made requests that were well out of his comfort zone. But a man's gotta eat. What is a man to do. A bat sailed through the air and then disappeared into the darkness again. He disliked the dark. He would much rather be out under the sun. When Chi had been Chirag, his mother would take him out to the beach. Those were his fondest memories. She died when he was 15. He disliked almost everything else about his childhood. His name had been the first thing to go. He had many names today. But only one that he had given himself. Chi. Chi like the Greek alphabet. But also, Chi the flow of universal energy when written down. And Chi pronounced Kai when spoken out. Chi as in the personal god for Igbo. His own destiny, Made with his own hands.

Onye kwe, Chi ya ekwe.

The others were daft bordering on the distasteful. G.S.K. Guitar String Killer. When he exclusively used Violin Strings in his Garrottes. Indians had always been unimaginative in the way they named people like him. Stoneman, Hammerman.

Artless.

The first time he had used the strings was on his father. The man had nothing to offer them but frustration and impotence. When Chi's mother did not get up that night, he could see the fear in his father's face. Chi had first broken his violin over his head and then finished him off with the strings. Synthetic core. But easier for a first timer. The man hadn't struggled against him. He was staring at the lifeless body of the woman he had abused for so long. Chi wasn't looking at her. He had more important things to do. It haunted him all the same.

God, grant me the serenity to accept the things I cannot change, courage to change the things I can, and wisdom to know the difference.

That was when he had found his passion. He checked the back door again. No movement. Chi was good at waiting. He opened his thermos and poured some coffee into the cup. The trick to it was to store it cold. Hot coffee killed itself after 5 minutes in a thermos. The only drink Chi disliked was Chai. Well, that and any type of Smoothie. At the edge of his consciousness, there was an irrefutable certainty that guided his hand. He knew that the Gods were with him. Only through God everything was permitted. He bowed his head and sighed.

Hare Ram Hare Ram, Ram Ram Hare Hare
Hare Krishna Hare Krishna Krishna Krishna Hare Hare

Inside his pockets he had two wound garrottes; one with catgut and one with metal. And a spare coil of synthetic string. He regularly oiled the gut strings with olive oil to extend their life. It also helped with the humidity. Gut strings tend to hold their quality nicely right up until they fail. Metal and Synthetic are more reliable but don't have the same aesthetic feel to them. Lately everything had been a little too high profile for his taste. There was nothing tasteful about shooting someone and fleeing the scene. He wanted to stand over the scene. Maybe even light a cigarette. Catch his breath. Wipe off his sweat. Clean up after him. Methodically retrace his steps back and vanish. He had to lie low for months after the last shootout. Something didn't sit right with him. It was his first time being paid in crypto. He didn't want to jinx it, and had ended up accepting the mark. The old fart never saw it coming. But then who does. He knew he wouldn't see it coming either. When it came.

He saw the man exit the building, fumbling around with the locks. Chi noiselessly climbed out of his car and began to move towards the mark like a tiger stalking his prey. The man began to make his way across the street to his car. Chi moved in between the shadows, finally coming to a stop. Without a breath.

Tch. Tch. Tch.

The man turned around in horror. Chi dragged him into the lightless alley with one strong pull, his other hand on the mark's mouth. Once he felt they couldn't be seen or heard, he took out the strings. Holding on to the man with an unbreakable grip on his throat with his left hand. In one swift movement, Chi had the man on the ground with the noose around his neck.

mīhar-r ināmhar-r ihāll ims-iB

And then he began to pull. Slowly at first. But firm. Unyielding. The man was trying to hit him with the back of his palms. Chi waited. He was good at waiting. He shifted his weight. The struggle was weaker now. Just at the edge. At the edge. The man attempted to turn his head around. Chi turned away. He disliked looking at their eyes. The mark finally stopped moving. Chi slowly unwound the string from his neck and carefully rolled it back before replacing it in his pocket. He pulled out a crumpled cigarette from his pocket and bit on it.

And so he goes with god.

Om Mani Padme Hum

The space of the symbolic

Writing on the Walls

Sometimes people say Quantum Mechanics is all wrong. When the uncertainty exceeds its bounds what happens to the wave train. Chain signifiers float untethered, and the axis of understanding decreases ever so slowly. In chalk and paint and posters the formulae that spelled the freedom of the oppressed and the emancipation of the crushed and were soon wiped off or painted over when the opportunity came. The market square is clean and empty now, with fresh paint on the walls. The streets are open and the graffiti on the roads was washed off by the rain and erased by the movement of endless black tires.

The space of the virtual

XLR8

New leads on Memetic Hyperstitions
Thursday May 24th 2027
Categories: Codex 784

I have procured fragments of the Parsani Documents. They are largely confused and unintelligible. Occasionally I find a string or a phrase that makes some sense, but the context around it resists all attempts at interpellation. The implosive nature of the field and the explosive nature of the goals of change should be reconcilable, but it isn't working. Resisting the constant reterritorialization of the field by Capital, Parsani's papers have no solution to that end as far as I can see. I would need to get my hands on more of his work before I can say anything conclusive.

It makes me reconsider the need for scientific addendums on the existing socio-cultural work that is being done. Inside these pages, and in all the samizdats is a need for something more empirical. I don't see how it will result in change, unless both these halves come together to form a whole. It is very rare for me to hold with something so disgustingly Hegelian, but I don't see any other alternatives. More of Parsani's work will certainly offer lines of flight out of the petrodollar dome, but it won't change the dominance of most other structures that hold total sway over the individual.

11 responses to "New leads on Memetic Hyperstitions"

Charulata Kween says:
May 24th 2027 4:54 p.m.

I have more of his notes if you are interested.

Narka XLR8, says:
May 24th 2027 5:23 p.m.

Would you be willing to mail them to me?

Charulata Kween, says:
May 24th 2027 5:23 p.m.

Ummm, No. But I can help you out if you're open to an exchange of information?

Narka XLR8, says:
May 24th 2027 5:24 p.m.

How so?

Charulata Kween, says:
May 24th 2027 5:24 p.m.

A copy of the text fragment that you have in exchange for the ones I do.

Narka XLR8, says:
May 24th 2027 5:25 p.m.

Hello CBI, Nice B8. What up?

Charulata Kween, says:
May 24th 2027 5:29 p.m.

Haha, Not really. No. Let's just say you're not the only one with an interest in Hyperstitions. I would like to meet IRL if you are open to it.

Narka XLR8, says:
May 24th 2027 5:37 p.m.

Progressive I hope?

Charulata Kween, says:
May 24th 2027 4:54 p.m.

Beyond such distinctions.

The space of the real

'Imagine your pain as a black ball of negative energy. Draw out the Habit from your fingertips, from your toes, from every part of your body and feel it coalescing in your gut in one spinning orb. And then pull it out of you. Hold it in your hand. Feel it, and then throw it out!' the woman flashed her big smile. Shark. Neha was sitting in the same row as him today. He had arrived first. He wanted to see what her reaction was to the woman, but he didn't want her to catch him staring. He wondered how much the speaker was being paid. Her 'treatment' was flexible enough to be applicable to everything, and consequently couldn't really be effective against anything. He could tell that she had flashed that smile at corporate seminars, at couple's retreats, at schools, colleges, polytechnics, half-filled seminar halls, abroad for astrology hoes, and domestically for kitty parties. She did not smile with her eyes. No Duchenne markers. He respected her a little. Hers was more convincing than his had ever been.

Neha did not smile. At least he had never seen her smile. She went through the motions, gave her speech, joined in the circle, but she was somewhere else. This was Vikram's fifth meeting. She had asked him to pass her the sachet at the last meeting. He'd passed it with an indifferent 'Here.' Those were the only words they'd exchanged. Some of the footage was always unusable. Neha's address was practiced. She had it down. Sometimes she'd change some of the details, but no one would catch her at it. He wouldn't have either, had he not gone over the footage and the audio at night after the meetings. How much of what she said was true?

Vikram turned over to look at her. She was staring straight ahead at empty space.

'And when the chakras align, the spirit is cleared and the flow of life can continue.' The way this woman spoke made him feel that her understanding of Eastern philosophy was rooted in children's cartoons. Whose wasn't these days? She was wrapping up the session. A few people flocked to her, while others were in a hurry to leave. Neha got up sluggishly, replacing her notebook in her satchel. He moved towards her. She clicked her jaw.

'Hey, Umm Neha right?' he said.

'Yeah. You're new?' she replied.

'No, I've been coming here for a month now.' He eyed her as she did the jaw thing again.

'You're new.'

'Well, I had a few questions, I was hoping you could help me out?'

'Fire away.'

'If you have the time, maybe we could sit down somewhere for a coffee.'

She considered it for a moment. 'Yeah, I've got an hour or two to kill.'

As they came out of the basement, the sun had just dipped under the buildings and the sky was a warm yellow. The sound of footsteps was coming from the centre circle. The middle circle was almost always empty. She pointed out the way with her thumb and started on the cobbled road. Vikram followed along. A lot of the shops were closed. And the smaller alleys that cut in between the circles were beginning to swell up with people holding vodkas and whiskey-scotch blends in paper cups under wispy but steady clouds of smoke.

'Where we headed?'

'There's this place around here somewhere I like, I can never keep it straight so we'll have to look around a little.'

Vikram nodded. They passed the trash collection point and Vikram turned to look at the graffiti. There was nothing there. The erasure committee was very efficient. At least when it came to street art that had any social relevance or was critical of the ruling party. Guthka stains and Political adverts always managed to escape the white washers. He remembered that the button camera was still recording; he turned it off and pocketed it. They passed by a second-hand bookshop and by the time they stopped at the sidewalk café even he didn't know exactly where he was. He followed her inside, and the barista immediately greeted her by name.

'So, what do you want to know?' she was shuffling through her satchel nervously.

'I've been listening to you at the meetings'

'Mmhmm,' she had taken out a pack and offered him one. He took one and waited for her to light hers.

'I used to admin a page as well'

'Mmhmm.'

'I gave it up eventually. I felt like I was flushing too much of my time down the drain. Some of my friends have had similar experiences, but nothing as extreme as yours.'

'Maybe I was just a little too fucked up before all of this, and this is how it came out to be' she smiled, forcefully blowing out smoke from her nose.

Vikram smiled uncomfortably. Maybe.

'No, so see I don't think mental health can be quantified that easily. It's different for different people. What I don't get is if you don't have the Habit, why are you attending the meetings at all?' she flicked her cigarette at the end of the sentence.

'I'm doing an article.'

'Oho, for your college newsletter?' she smirked.

'Ha-ha, No. I freelance for some magazines.'

'Fancy.'

'Have you struggled with any other addictions?'

'Not really'

Their coffees arrived. He opened the demerara and helped himself to a generous amount of it. He could feel her eyes on him, staring in silent judgement. Maybe he should not have put the camera away.

'While you fixate on addictions Vikram, you fail to take into account everything that has changed in the world' she was looking away thoughtfully sipping on her iced latte.

She turned back to him 'The same idea is making its way into every other place. This obsessive need to be endlessly productive.'

Vikram thought back to the unfinished reels in his room. The week sometimes month-long searches for the perfect piece of music. His need to churn out more work, better work than those around him. He wasn't 'wasting' his time online like many others, but he was still in the productivity mill.

'See, that's all there is to it' she smiled.

The sun had gone down, the neon from the stores and the white streetlights had sparked up all around them. Vikram decided he might as well come clean to her about himself and the documentary.

The space of the dream

In the silent night of the tathagata loneliness at a motel pool displaced in time and place, two kids look out at the galaxy tilted in the middle of the water.

The space of the real

'Sometimes I have these dreams where I am drowning endlessly. I keep falling through the water but I never hit bottom. I have tried to move through it, to reach some surface. But I never can. There is no up or down. The pressure never changes. It never gets darker or brighter. And whatever direction I was moving in, the moment I stop struggling – I start falling in the opposite direction. It is oppressive. Endless. Dark. When you fall in your dreams from something a building, a balancing wire, or a plane, you hit bottom and then you wake up. But I cannot wake up from these. I feel stifled like on the edge of a yawn. There is air going through me, but it never feels enough.' Navya had a pained look on her face. Torsha hadn't seen her this rattled in months.

'That's fucked up.'

'I know'

'Really fucked up.'

'I know'

'Navya, you need to get over this "I'll fix myself" bullshit. I have friends who see therapists and I'm sure we could get a good recommendation. Something that would suit you.'

'No.' she said, her eyes resolute.

'Babe . . .'

'No, Torsha. You know what it was like. I've had my share of brown sofas and snooty women looking down on me for hours on end. We both have. You should understand that better than anyone.'

'I do. I really do.'

'Do you?'

'Yes. But then it did work for me. It can work for you too Navs.' She pressed. Her sister needed the push. Ever since they were kids, even before their mom had passed away, Navya just had this thing where she would bury her head in the sand and pretend everything was all right no matter how bad things got.

'I don't even know why I tell you things. I don't want a shrink recommendation. I just need you to listen.'

'I am listening. Always have, always will.'

'Nevermind. I shouldn't have brought it up.'

'Okay okay, No more psych talk.' Torsha forced a pained smile. It was killing her. She knew better than to push her sister. The more you startled her, the more she closed herself off to everything. Navya liked to think that her spirit animal was a fox or an owl, but all she could see was a Hedgehog when she looked at her.

'No more psych talk.' she said softly.

'Things at the office, okay?'

'Okay. Manageable even. But not good.'

'You can always leave. You don't have to keep putting yourself through this.'

'Leave and go where? And do what?' Torsha could feel her sister's anxiety bubbling over.

'Anything. I'm not going to presume to tell you what it is that you do or are capable of doing even, but I know you have options. More than most people do. You don't owe any one anything.'

'I like the work Toto. Everything else just disappears into the background. The neuropsychological implications of the work I'm doing are immense. Enough to establish something lasting. But there's no department in any Uni in the country that has the resources that come even close to DOMA. The Chief deals with the ethics committee, and I can do what I need to in peace.'

'You won't ever be happy. If you keep going on like this.'

'Happiness is for the dull and the dumb.'

'Yes, because finding happiness in the small and everyday things automatically makes me dumb.'

'I'm not calling you dumb Toto'

'Feels like it.'

'Well, I'm not.'

'Hmm.'

'I don't understand how to get through to you Navya. Every day I try and every day it feels like it's just falling short of working.'

'If you really wanted that Toto, you wouldn't be forcing me to tie myself down here with you.'

'Navya, I'm not forcing you to do anything. You can leave tomorrow if you want.'

'You know I won't.'

'And I'm grateful for that. I don't know how I would make it alone out here. But that does not mean you get to bring that out and smack me with it, every time we're disagreeing on something.'

'Hmm.'

'It's only a few more years. I know this. You know this. Then if you want to tear this place down, I'll gladly stand by you and see the wrecking ball do the work. But only after he has passed on. Not a day before.'

'Who knows how long that will be? I feel like a part of my life has been put on permanent hold and there's nothing I can do about it.'

'No Navya, It hasn't been. I manage to have a life outside of everything. And I live here the same as you. So this place, him, none of these things have anything to do with you not living your life. Stop using them as a crutch.'

'Things aren't as easy for everyone as they are for you.'

'I know babe. But I'm here. I've always been. Mum wouldn't like to see us like this.'

'It doesn't matter what she would or wouldn't like. The dead have no preferences.'

'Navya . . .'

'It's okay, I'm sorry. I just don't feel good enough. I'm going to go to bed early.'

Torsha nodded, projecting sympathy on her face. The truth was she was tired of this, this routine. Navya got up and left her room, leaving the door open behind her.

The space of the virtual

Based
/beɪst/

Verb

1. Strongly Agree
2. Used to signal approval and recognition for a person being real
3. Not Cringe / Cringen't

Example 1: Meta-Ironic or Moronic

OP: Based.
SP: Based on what?

Example 2: Political (Possibly Anti-Political)

OP: That snivelly alt-righter just got trolled off brit tele by the archbishop of
    banterbury
SP: Based

Example 3: Inquisitive (Possibly Rhetorical)

OP: Thinking of evading my taxes and becoming ungovernable
SP: Umm, Based?

Example 4: Post-Ironic

OP: I'm thinking about ending my life to lower my carbon foot-
print
SP: Hmm. Same. Based tho.

Example 5: Sincere

OP: The Bald Billionaire's capsule burned out on re-entry from space, got footage of the
    wreckage from liveleak, dm if you wanna see
SP: Based.

Example 6: Ironic

OP: So you see, given the choice between gamer girl piss or cow piss, I'd always go for the
    former.
SP: Yeah buddy, Based of you.

Example 7: Meta - Meta - Ironic

OP: I am going to commit war crimes after lunch.
SP: Based.

The space of the symbolic

Her voice was sweeter than sin. The undying embers still mark its flame. Her voice had faded but her wants had not. She knew at first sight - he would be the death of her.

And when his uneasy eyes and unearthly lips formed these words: 'I will die before you have me.'

'Have me' was all she could say.

She watched him drown into the silvery depths of himself, reflecting to him his own last words:

'Farewell.'

All that remains of them now is a flower that blooms only to hang its head in shame and an endless Echo.

The space of the real

As Pavan and Anamika drove across Delhi, he felt oddly amused. It had been years since they'd last been on a drive together. He could detect her perfume, but it was very faint. She had changed it. Not the only thing that had changed, he suspected. Her dark circles had retained their pinkish hue. Everything about her felt on edge – Jittery, Anxious, Uncertain. He almost felt like steering left and taking her to their little café that was a few kilometres from where they were. She was taking him to her new place.

'I don't understand' he could see her staring straight ahead into the distance.

'Mmhmm?' Pavan checked the GPS on his phone.

'I don't understand how the two connect.' Anamika rubbed her eyes.

'I can't help you with that unless you tell me more', he looked at the old decaying office buildings on the right. Everything she had told him about D.O.M.A. made his head spin.

'There is nothing more to tell. They're working on a way to essentially incept ideas inside people's heads. What I don't get is why all the puzzles.'

'Anamika . . .' he paused. 'Have you considered the possibility that they might have cooked up a fool's errand for you?'

'If they are willing to go this far just to keep little old me occupied, that just means there is something worth hiding, somewhere.'

'There's already enough thought control in the daylight . . .' he entered a circular intersection, turning slowly.

'I know'

'So why then?'

'Because as effective as it might be, it isn't total.' she said. 'Take a left here.'

He scanned the road ahead. Pavan felt a little sad that he no longer knew where she lived. But then again, she hadn't known where he lived until a few days ago either. 'It might not be total, but isn't that better. That little space serves as a justification for more vitriol.' he wondered out loud.

'Look, I don't know why they are doing it Pavan. I just know that they are.'

'Anamika, even if all of that is true. Where does Vijlandi come in or for that matter the Uqbari?'

'As I just said, I don't know.' the frustration in her voice was becoming more pronounced. He decided not to press her any further. They came on a road lined with Amaltas. He parked in the spot she'd pointed out.

'It's nice' he said.

'Yeah, I moved in last year, couldn't take the roommates anymore' she replied with an easy smile.

'You know, it's hard not to take that personally' Pavan felt lighter on his feet. He started climbing behind her, and felt sorrier and sorrier that things were over between them. The stairs were old and worn down, the walls were coming apart from the damp but the place felt warm and homely. Pavan smiled and looked up at Anamika as they reached her door. She was frozen in place. Her face had gone white. Pavan gave her an inquisitive look. She pointed at her door lock. It was open.

Pavan placed his hand on her shoulder and pulled her away from the door. The place was a mess. Pavan had a feeling that all the documents that she wanted him to see were long gone by now. There were papers scattered across her living room. The drawers had been tossed. He opened the door to her bedroom and walked in. It was the only room that looked untouched.

A sudden movement behind him caught his attention. Before

he could do anything a heavy blow to his head knocked him down. He felt his legs go from under him. Pavan fell to his knees and then felt his face hit the ground. As the warm blood trickled down from the base of his skull, he tried to turn his head up. He felt he would pass out from the blinding pain any second now. The man was turning over a metal wire in his hand. Pavan could see a blur that looked like a gun tucked in his jeans. Pavan felt like smiling at the unceremonious end he was about to meet but his facial muscles refused to move. The man placed his boot on his neck and pressed down.

He felt like his lungs were on fire. He clutched at the boot, trying to get it off him. But his arms felt weaker with every passing moment. A trickle of blood had forced him to close one of his eyes. The man tightened the grip on the wire and bent down. Pavan heard a big crashing sound and then everything went dark.

The space of the symbolic

The bloodied arcade game stands in the centre of the public square on a raised platform. Blood dripping down from the buttons. The corpse of the last player is being dragged away as the rest of the accused stand in a line waiting their turn.

They have a slim chance at life if they beat the game. Most don't. The Machine punishes indiscriminately and cleans up what is left. The guards don't take any pleasure in their work. But they are happy to not be the ones who have to drag the mangled bodies away.

The space of the dream

When did 'I' come here? 'I' remember walking around the trails. 'I' remember the rivulets that divide the landscape, the way the cliff side looks under the first rays of the sun.

The sound of the ocean crashing against the shoreline brings something forgotten to the tip of the tongue that never finds articulation. The ruins make me think that the place served as a temporary port in the past. The people who lived here are not people anymore but actions. They residually haunt the island – the shattered remains of their lives tracing themselves out endlessly. As 'I' walk over the sand, the ghosts of the people who were shipwrecked here walk with me. 'I' find it increasingly hard to remember things about my life. Some hazy details float in and out, but as soon as 'I' try to hold on to them, they fall to pieces. The fragments float off and vanish into nothingness. Nothing can grow in the ashes of forgetting. And if something manages to, the malcontent will choke anyone who breathes in the air.

'I' am as empty and changing as the ocean around me.

How did 'I' end up here?

The space of the real

Inside the endless maze

Neha looked at Vikram as he stopped in front of a closed shutter. They were a little ways away from the bridal stores and the cafes.

The alleys here were filled with hardware shops, tailors, cheap eateries, and the people of Shahpur Jat. Vikram was insincere and flimsy when it came to most things. But never when it came to her – she liked that about him.

'You know it's rude to stare'

'A little impoliteness never harmed anyone.'

The empty hallways alive with footsteps

The janitor looked up and saw the man making his way across the main hall. He should have said something, but decided not to. They didn't pay him enough to be a hero. There was nothing to be gained by angering a man who had managed to break inside the main complex and bypass two levels of security.

It takes two to do anything. . .

'You're the most beautiful girl in this bar.' She looked at the guy, not bad. She could do worse. And she had.

'I'm not even in the top five.'

'Insecure and hot, my kinda woman.'

'Did you unironically just say that.'

'I am always sincere.'

'Always?'

'Well, almost always.'

'Well, why don't we start small, what is the name of the most beautiful girl in the bar who doesn't even think she's in the top five.'

'Navya.'

On this side of the glass, evening has already fallen

The essence of the alchemical creed is the search for the truth within the truth. The Accelerationist cause has had to dodge them at every turn – there's conspiracy theory paranoid and then there's alchemist paranoid. At every turn, some study group or the other would stumble on the latest cybernetic theory and try to distort it to their own pseudoscientific ends.

In the past year alone the local circle in Delhi had to dispatch people to recover documents from the "students." Their work was never-ending.

On the road

'Fuck. Fuck. Fuck. Fuck.'

'Kill me please.'

'You're not dead yet. But you came real close.'

'What happened? My head is killing me.'

'You got knocked out, with a souvenir crystal jar. Lucky for you, I keep a baseball bat in the living room.'

'Who was he?'

'Who the fuck knows. Supari killer, Private contractor – It doesn't matter. I'm sorry Pavan. I didn't mean to drag you into this.'

'Okay I'm going to pass out now. Let me know when we get wherever the fuck you're taking me.'

'Don't pass out on a head injury idiot. Sit up, keep talking to me.'

In a lowly bar that will remain nameless

He had missed his check-in. Shit. This was the third time Chi had missed the check-in this year. Wonder where that son of a bitch was passed out now.

For the third time tonight

'Tired already? Want to go sleep?' Torsha smiled at him. The best way to get a guy to keep going was to taunt him.

'No, are you?'

'Not just yet.' She grabbed his hair and pushed his head under the sheets.

There are bars on the windows

The clouds were cutting in and out of the hotel's window. The view was warped, suburban, and dull; a small river and a highway that cut over it. And endless maze of apartment buildings in the distance. He really disliked hotels that had bars on the windows. What was the point in having stylish sliding windows if you couldn't even feel the breeze without being assaulted by the iron bars.

'Come back to bed, why are you at the window?' he turned back and looked at Torsha.

'Nothing just had a bad dream.' Karna closed the window and went back to bed.

How the Beggar man found Tinker and Tailor

Jatin adjusted his kambal and nestled in deeper into his corner on the footpath. He had been woken up by the sounds of the men arguing. They were arguing about murder. He knew they knew that he was there on the footpath – Sleeping or Half Awake. He knew they didn't care what he overheard. People like him were invisible. And he wanted to stay that way.

The space of the dream

The Cartography of Emptiness

The map maker sits alone in his room at the end of time and

draws up and marks out the nothingness all around him. He marks every non-being that moves or stays still and gives meaning to all the signs that point endlessly to other signs that point to other signs to other signs to other signs to other signs.

The Calculus of Separation

The bookcase in front of her was half empty. The remaining books had fallen over. The outlines were still visible in the dust that had settled before they had been picked off. She wanted to reach out and knock the whole thing over, but didn't.

The Topology of Ecstasy

The curves that disconnect the one into the two, and spaces that can be deformed into one and into the other and back again without loss. The local flatness of the emotion then carries over or is itself a reduction of the manifold – determining when, how and where the collapse will occur when they touch each other.

The Mechanics of Angst

Simple machines of dread that are connected to each other and constrained by their connections. Kinematic pairs of dread that connect to other simple machines of dread that connect to other simple machines endlessly. Complex machines of Dread. Complex machines that look at each other and feel dread. Complex machines that look at themselves and feel dread. Complex machines that look at the night sky and feel dread.

The Algebra of Misery

When you add and square and root the reminders of the things that aren't there, the things that you know were there once and never will be there again, the things that were never there but are reminders in their not-being-thereness, the things that you thought will be there but aren't – what is left? What is the remainder? The x at the end of the equation that stares at the solution on the other side of those two parallel lines.

The Combinatorics of Greif

Enumerate for me the ways in which you look at your time together. Generate functions. Graph it for me. Show me the countably infinite ways, the chains that link the random walks of madness that define the problem of us.

The space of the real

On and on it went with her. The lies. One after the other. Lies inside lies inside lies inside lies. You never knew if you were at the last matryoshka layer of what it was that had happened. Of what was happening. There was no NDA, not even a simple three sentence agreement that was keeping her from telling him what had happened. She just chose not to. Or rather she preferred not to as she would put it. It was on their third meeting after he had told her about his work that she finally name dropped D.O.M.A. Vikram tried to read in between the lines, to pick up scraps when she wasn't being careful with what she said. He could tell that the outlines of whatever had happened were more than your usual run of the mill job trauma and the way her voice got shaky whenever she started talking about the place was deeply unsettling. So, he let it be, for now.

Her whole thing as it were rested on this damaged but badass aura that she gave off. But whenever he spoke to her at length, he could see a little behind the veil. But who knew really? There were days when he felt more exposed behind the camera than anything in front of it could ever be. There was something about her that resisted being named. She had taken it upon herself to help him out with his work and refused to take no for an answer. He had already gotten everything he could from the meets. But there was more to Neha, and that was all he really cared about. They were walking around the meeting areas today under the pretence of taking establishing shots; something that he greatly disliked and almost never used in his work. He liked spending time with her. It was getting harder to tell where the line was, if there was one anymore. 'I've always liked this graffiti here' Vikram turned around. It was a hastily painted silhouette of two girls holding hands. 'There used to be more around the area but most of them either got painted over with officially commissioned "street art" or just whitewashed.'

'I have some of it on film somewhere.' One of his first projects had started out with him stitching together vignettes of graffiti with shaky shots of colonial buildings.

'I would love that.' she gave him a tired smile.

'I'll have to hunt around for it a while but I'll mail it to you.'

'Or I could come by your place and I can finally see that projector keep raving about.'

'I don't rave, come on.'

'It's good Vikram.' she touched her watch. 'Good to have something you're passionate about.'

'You never talk about that you know, what you're passionate about.'

'I'll let you know when I find out if I ever do.'

The space of the virtual

About Nothing

Scene 1

An orchard in Messina circa. 2021

Benedict.   My Dear Lady Disdain! Are you yet living?

Beatrice.   He screams for he does not know.

Benedict.   Who are you, who are so wise in the ways of
               science?

Beatrice.   Oh don't mind me. No thoughts, Head Empty.

Benedict.   You know, I'm something of a scientist myself.

Beatrice.   The ability to speak does not make you intelligent.

Benedict.   Why so serious?

Beatrice.   Bold of you to assume it's seriousness and not
               disdain. Why have you chosen to darken this
               grove?

Benedict.   It's free real estate. Besides, I thought I'd get this
               bread.

Beatrice.   That's the neat part. You don't.

Benedict.   I find your lack of faith disturbing.

Beatrice.   Strange isn't it?

Benedict.   Only a sith deals in absolutes.

Beatrice.   You went full retard. Never go full retard.

Benedict.   Okay, so basically I'm monkey?

Beatrice.   The law requires that I answer 'No.'

Benedict.   That wasn't very cash money of you.

Beatrice.   Can I offer you an egg in this trying time?

Benedict.   Yare Yare Daze. That's a lot of damage.

Beatrice.   Next you'll say I was only pretending to be
              retarded.

Benedict.   Why would you say something so controversial
              yet so brave?

Beatrice.   What is man? A miserable pile of secrets.

Benedict.   It really do be like that sometimes.

Beatrice.   This is what zero pussy does to MF.

Benedict.   You know at first I was like "Mmm Feet" as a joke.
              But bro I don't think that's a joke anymore.

Beatrice.   That will age like milk. I need some Unsee juice
              now.

Benedict.   Your boos mean nothing to me, I've seen what makes you cheer.

Beatrice.   Ara Ara, Ladies and gentlemen. We got him.

Benedict.   So you're telling me there's a chance?

Beatrice.   Fuck around and find out.

Benedict.   Hey don't @ me. I guess it's true what they say Hoes mad.

Beatrice.   Oh, I'm die now.

Benedict.   Don't kill yourself, you're so sexy aha. Just kidding . . . Unless?

Beatrice.   Outstanding move. But, wait. That's illegal. Plague be upon ye.

Benedict.   (shrugging) Gaslight. Gatekeep. Girlboss.

Beatrice.   Guys literally only want one thing and it's fucking disgusting.

Benedict.   Alright, We'll call it a draw. I'll be honest. I don't wanna be horny anymore, I wanna be happy.

Beatrice.   Weird Flex but okay.

Benedict.   It is rather Based isn't it.

Beatrice.   Based? Based on what?

Benedict.   I am sick of crying, tired of trying, yes I'm smiling but inside I'm dying.

Beatrice.   (whispers) I can fix him.

                        Curtain.

Scene 2

A room in Leonato's house.

(A mysterious message coming from nowhere)

Let me in. Let me in. LET ME IN!!!!!!!!!!

Enter Hamlet Sr.

Benedict.   Eat my ass spirits.

Beatrice.   Only the dead can know peace from this evil.

Benedict.   I've seen enough hentai to know where this is
                 going.

Hamlet.   I summon you to fulfil your oath.

Beatrice.   Major Persona vibes.

Benedict.   Poetic Cinema.

Beatrice.   What is this a crossover episode?

Benedict.   Fuck off ghost. (to Hamlet Sr.) I thought you were
                 dead

Hamlet.   The details of my death were greatly exaggerated.

Benedict.   (sighing) That's how mafia works.

Beatrice.   Where is your God now?
Benedict.   Reject tradition, Embrace modernity.

Beatrice.   Uhm, cheesed to meet you. What's the plan
               Mr. Sandman?

Benedict.   It's time to duel.

Hamlet.   You disengenous dense motherfucker. I'm here
             for the money.

Benedict.   Oh no, Anyway . . .

Hamlet.   Omae wa mou shindeiru.

Benedict.   Nani.

Agent.   FBI Open Up!

Enter Agent.

Agent.   Stop right there, Criminal scum. (cuffing Hamlet)
            Ladies and gentlemen we got him.

Hamlet.   Is this some sort of peasant joke that I'm too rich
             to understand?

Benedict.   You may have outsmarted me, but I outsmarted
               your outsmarting.

Hamlet.   I will look for you. I will find. And I will kill you.

Beatrice.   Well that escalated quickly.

Curtain.

Scene 3

A street.

Benedict.   Do you think God lives in heaven because he too
             lives in fear of what he's created?

Beatrice.   Be not afraid, We can just attack and dethrone
             God.

Benedict.   Yeah, If you could stop doing that. That'd be great.

Beatrice.   Not all heroes wear capes.

Benedict.   We'll bang, OK? Thick thighs save lives.

Beatrice.   Best I can do is friendship. Press F to pay respects.

Benedict.   (headpats) What if it was all just a dream? What a
             time to be alive.

Beatrice.   Ugh fine, I guess you are my pogchamp. Come
             here.

Curtain.

The space of the symbolic

As a conclusion to your Training take the following test to assess your understanding of the material:

Part A

Select the option that you think best answers the question. There can be more than one right answer.

1. What are the attitudes that best define an ideal employee at our company?

A. Compliance and Agreeableness
B. Compliance and Subservience
C. Compliance and Acquiescence
D. Compliance and Sycophancy

2. The correct response to a manager when they ask you 'How did you find the work this week' is?

A. I loved it, it was challenging and enjoyable. I love entering data into excel sheets.
B. It was wonderful, I love that I was given the opportunity to organise the emails today
C. I am so excited about reconciling the contact information for ten thousand clients
D. All of the above

3. When you see an employee trying to start a union and discussing their wages to see if they are being paid the same as the

other genders, You:

A. Explain to them how they are being insensitive to the company and their behaviour can be triggering for the Management
B. Explain to them that this is a family and not a company, and they have no right to start any trouble here
C. Both A and B
D. Report them to the Line Manager

4. When asked about the company's work environment by an outsider, the correct way to Respond to them is:

A. It is a great environment, I love being given the opportunity to become an internal stakeholder in such a prestigious corporation.
B. It is a great environment, I love being given the opportunity to become an internal stakeholder in such a prestigious corporation.
C. It is a great environment, I love being given the opportunity to become an internal stakeholder in such a prestigious corporation.
D. It is a great environment, I love being given the opportunity to become an internal stakeholder in such a prestigious corporation.

5. What are your feelings about the company? (The space is left blank, please devise your own options and select the one you feel best represents what you feel)

A.
B.
C.
D.

Part B

Select the option that best completes the blanks left in the sentences. There can be more than one right answer

6. ________ the public sentiment against the CEO, the company didn't have to pay any taxes.

A. Because of
B. Thanks to
C. Despite
D. Using

7. The CEO is a true ________, the incidental fact that ________ has no relation with ________.

A. Visionary, his family owned emerald mines, his wealth
B. Genius, he didn't invent the things he's selling, how he forced the original inventors out
C. Philanthropist, he got tax breaks for it, his selfless contribution
D. Pacifist, he supported a coup for lithium where thousands died, his commitment to world peace

8. The number one threat to the company's future is ________.

A. Trade Unions
B. Time Theft
C. Human Rights Watch
D. Sexual Harassment Lawsuits

9. Employees are expected to come to work to ________, and

not to _________.

A. Work, have fun
B. Work, earn
C. Create surplus value, expect "handouts"
D. To survive, make a living

10. The company has a 0 tolerance policy for _________.

A. Twitches
B. Glitches
C. Booze
D. All of the above

Your results will be sent to you, by email. If you do not pass the test, you can retake it as many times as you need to.

The space of the real

She was certain that it was in a dream where she first saw the two of them together. He was climbing a dusty staircase with broken steps. There were no railings and the doors of some of the apartments were repurposed tin roofing hanging shabbily on their hinges. As he clattered up the steps, an old man opens the door in his face and grumbles out in his rough voice with something entirely Slavic in it. 'What are you doing here?' What is he doing here? There is nothing that he can say that would satisfy him. She poked her head in from the upper flight, 'He is with me.'

    The confidence and severity in her voice sends the old man

back inside his flat. He climbed up to her and asked why she had invited him there. They entered an apartment that he knew couldn't be hers. The things inside belonged to a happy family. The carpet would scream if it had a mouth, so he took care to avoid stepping on it as he walked around the place. She beckoned him to follow her to the balcony.

The soft wind hits his face all at once; cool and blue. She pointed to the courtyard down below. It was covered in tarmac from end to end. Some white chairs lying about with reckless abandon. On the right, beyond the fence, a heavy thicket of trees and shrubbery blocking the view and on the left, the ocean spills into the courtyard.

Navya lit her first cigarette of the day as she leaned against the railing of the overhead bridge. She had her back to him. The traffic under the bridge was beginning to thin out. He pulled out one and lit it, letting his hand slowly fall to his side. Navya saw the edge of his kurta flapping in the wind, burning in places where it brushed against the cigarette. She let the smoke out in a sigh and watched it dissolve into nothingness.

'How is she these days?'

He said nothing for a while. 'The same as usual I suppose. I haven't been paying attention to her'

'You will have all the time in the world for that soon.' She said blowing the smoke through her hand, turning it against the light coming from the platform.

'Hmm' he leaned in right next to her. 'He must be happy?'

Was he happy? The more Navya thought about it, the more certain she grew that none of them were really happy. But there was no need to say anything more than the bare minimum today. She didn't want to end things on a note that would make the memory more painful than it needed to be.

'I suppose so.' She watched a beggar girl climb the divider below to get to her mother on the other side. 'I think he has always suspected.' She added without really meaning to.

'And said nothing?'

'It's not in his nature. I think he believes that if he denies it strongly enough inside himself it'll stop being true.'

'Do you think she knows?'

'You tell me.'

'I can't read her.' He scratched his head thoughtfully with his thumb, the smoke dangerously close to his eyes.

Navya felt uncharacteristically sentimental but decided not to let anything she was feeling show on her face.

'You don't have to go you know. I can leave her. You can leave him. We could move to a new city; a new city that has no stale memories for either of us.'

She turned to face him. She wasn't expecting him to say so much so soon. From the look on his face, she could tell that he hadn't wanted to say it either.

'Things fall apart all the time to make way for new things.'

'Yes.' His voice had regained its detached coolness. She felt the knot that had formed in her chest loosen. She turned her head away from him again. It would be easier for them to keep up their pretences like that. The eyes, said more than either of them wanted.

Navya wondered if her boyfriend had hoped that if they changed cities, this would end. He was right, this was ending. But she knew that it wasn't going to fix anything between them. How soon before something new started in Bangalore? And what if she stayed but left both of them anyway? Her sister needed her more than either of them. Maybe her boyfriend and the man who was standing next to her both were really just details; unimportant details that orbited her life.

She wanted this to mean something more. She wanted it to be enough for her to justify her actions to herself. But it wasn't. And there was nothing that she could do to convince herself otherwise.

'Why him?' he moved in closer to her, his elbow brushed lightly against hers.

'Would it be horrible if I said Habit?' she turned to look at his eyes. They were fixed unmovably on the empty pavement down below.

'It's comfortable' she continued. 'I don't have to think about anything when I am with him. Everything is out of habit. I like not thinking about these things. It is comfortable. If we went through what you're suggesting it would turn into a big mess. And by the time it will all be over, whatever we have. Whatever this is would also have faded out.' She shifted her weight on her other foot. 'Isn't this better? Cleaner? Simpler?'

'That it is.'

She cocked her head to one side, wondering if it would have been better to have avoided this altogether.

'Come, let's go someplace else.'

'Where?'

'Anywhere but here.' She didn't want to spend another second here, in this spot. Something was bubbling inside her, and she could already feel the place dying for her.

When they boarded the metro, she didn't look back.

The space of the symbolic

Dialectics of Propaganda

To begin with, there is a thing. Then because of the thingness of that thing and because of how we think in binaries or spectrums that move from one end to another, you have the anti-thing. Now that we have the thing and the anti-thing, what do we do with them?

Let them annihilate each other? Be content with the photons and the fermions that remain? Let there be light? But then you're left with the asymmetry. What to do with the imbalance. So, you let things go a little further, to see how they play out. Now you have a new thing. And because you have a new thing, by the law of binary spectrums, you will have the anti-new thing. Which will give you the new new thing. And on and on and on until the thingness of things and the anti-thingness of anti-things stretches out into infinities – both positive and negative. Or is it an internal look at the thingness of things, where these back and forths lead to the true thing.

In a given year, somewhere in the world someone says something. Adding a little feather to the tiresome burden of "world knowledge," to settle the imbalance someone else adds something else. In a given year, someone looks at what it was that was added, and adds it themselves to their place and time, to their here and now. But the clever beast knows, that someone else will add something else. The clever beast does not know who that someone else is, but they know what that something else is. So, to offset it, he adds the counteractive to it beforehand. The remedy is administered before the symptoms have the time to show themselves.

In a given year, somewhere in the world someone utters non-truths with ferocity and speed and with diction that bullies and intimidates the Other into silence. In another given year, somewhere else in the world someone changes the nouns in the sentence and imitating the ferocity and the speed and the diction, bullies and intimidates some other Other into silence.

In any given year, when you look at the things said in their here and now, and in your here and now, is your here and now the result of their here and now from a few years back or is it the result of your here and then that itself was once a here and now that was a result of their here and now or perhaps their here and now is a result of the then and there that was once truly yours and is now unknown to you except through the lens of their then and there.

In any given year, whose lies are being fed to you? What will you do when the lies that you are sipping are shoddy rip-offs. With a few letters rearranged here and there, to avoid an outright intellectual property infringement. What will you do when the ways of lying are the same? Will you sit in the same silence?

Or will the silence you know be different somehow?

The space of the real

In the darkness of his room, Karna looked at the words floating around in the dim light of his laptop that was cracked in the upper right hand corner. The crack propagated from there and made its way to the upper left corner and the bottom right corner. The bottom left corner was untouched.

'You understand all of this?' Torsha leaned over him and looked at the communication between him and people whom Karna referred to as accelerationists.

'Barely.' Karna ran a blog. That was the extent of his involvement with them. But the way they were talking about this, this new thing they were after; their sincerity unnerved him. He couldn't tell if it was an extended elaborate shitpost that he was on the other end of, or people actually seeking ways to the singularity. And through government research?

'That guy there is disgusting.' Karna looked at the username that she was pointing at.

'Haha, yeah certainly not a guy you want to sic the cuss word bot on.'

'You have strange friends.'

'Less friends, and more strangers on the internet that I don't want to meet irl any day of the week.'

'So, what they're after is . . . some form of social control.' Torsha had a disgusted look on her face.

'Basically.'

'Typical. Men and their hobbies.'

'Gots to change the world, start wars and commit war crimes. It just do be like that sometimes.'

'Unhunh.' She leaned in close to his face. 'I hope you don't turn out to be a psycho.'

'Jury's out.'

'Despair springs eternal.' she threw herself back on his bed, exhausted.

'It looks like they're looking for ways to influence opinions through repeated exposure to certain forms of media.'

'That's an old invention Karna, it's called propaganda.'

'No, but this is different. What they're talking about looks like it's more invasive, more total somehow.'

'It says here "a repeated exposure to the stimuli would enforce compliance" and later on "the new media, while saturated still presents us with a lot of opportunities" Then there's some stuff about mimesis and replication that I can't really understand.'

'Why are they even operating on the surface web?' Torsha turned to Karna. But the word that he had said stuck with her – Mimesis. The only other place she had heard it spoken was between her sister and her grandfather.

'I suppose it's like hiding a tree in a forest. Between the endless conspiracy theorists and lore nuts, No one is really going to be paying enough attention to what is said in any one particular board.'

'Unhunh' she stopped herself from yawning out loud. He went back to reading the threads in silence. She could see things were already beginning to settle into a stale pattern between the two of them. As they always did. You find someone, get to know them. The spark in their eyes draws you to them like a moth to a flame, and then after a few weeks, you realise that there is nothing else to them. Just that one obsession that drives them, and occupies all their living hours. Her sister was no different. But then again, she hadn't really expected much from her sister. She was thankful for her little attempts at everyday empathy. She couldn't let herself be absorbed into something as completely as other people could. She disliked stagnation. She disliked the narrow depths of stale ponds that people picked for themselves and then spent all their time in. Letting it haunt their every stray thought. While being oblivious to the people around them. What their needs were.

The space of the symbolic

The association of dead people

The association existed to aid people in their fights against the Kafkaesque nightmare.

The system was fond of declaring people dead and then letting their land and property make their way into the pockets of the local Zameendars, and their votes into the pockets of their local parties. But the new president had bigger plans for the association of the dead. Mr. Chitra Gupta understood that the dead in the land of the living were not just limited to those who had been declared dead on paper while they were living. He understood that there were people who were dead inside but made play at living in order to convince themselves that they still were, there were people who were dead inside but put in the effort to live not for themselves but for the people in their lives. Then there were those who were so convinced of their vitality, that they never noticed that parts of them had died long ago and that other appendages were on the brink of falling off. Mr. Gupta understood that there were more dead among the living than there were in the land of the dead. And the association needed more sub-departments to address the issue. At least on a state level, he couldn't speak for the national or the international offices.

The space of the virtual

Quick Snap News

An aspiring foot model was found shot dead inside her car in a Mumbai alley over the weekend — less than a week after her parents reported her missing, a report said.

*

Vasirajus, the edutech giant has filed defamation lawsuits against prominent student activists and teachers' unions who have been protesting their allegedly unlawful modes of coercing students and parents into opting for their programs. The "unicorn" start-up recently filed for bankruptcy despite high initial valuations.

*

Three Dalit children were beaten to death after they were found using the playground that has been historically reserved for the local Brahmin children – the sarpanch to visit the grieving families.

*

The oil spill in Indian Ocean caused last month by Credence, the multinational conglomerate is now on fire.

_ _ _ Log in to see more.

The space of the real

For months she couldn't get the images out of her head. The images weren't one but many. Every horror is a distorted multiplicity. What was floating inside her head felt that it was generated by a subpar LLM and not by her own mind. Things had been better for her for the past few weeks. They felt more settled. Manageable.

Deeply affected by any stimuli, in the first few months, she had escaped through meditation, Tibetan incense and uncountable cups of chamomile. The meetings were a good distraction. A convenient mask to wear in a room filled with people with masks of their own. She didn't believe in weighing her misery against that of others. However, being in a room filled with people with problems less serious than her own was a great source of relief. She wanted to be one of them, someone whose problems were lighter. And against everything it worked. Slowly she found herself looking at things in a different light. She had succeeded in doing to herself what for years the Department had been unable to achieve with its subjects. It wasn't a big success but a small one. She was grateful for it. As long as there were ways for her to exist that made life more liveable, she would continue to be.

It was a wonder that she had stumbled onto Vikram. Here was someone who held the promise of something more than a distraction. She looked at everyone she met and tried to keep something of them with her. The way they moved out of the way or how they turned a corner. For Vikram, it was this maniacal gleam in his eye and the shakiness in his voice that started slow but kept on rising in intensity as he rambled on about some detail in some film or the other that he really liked. She didn't like films. There was very little music that was palatable for her. She read, but in sporadic bursts that were capped on both ends by weeks of not reading a single sentence. But she loved to listen to people talking about the things they were passionate about. Being with them was a little like being in a room full of strangers who had different problems. Neha hoped to feel a little of the passion they felt for their things through them.

The space of the dream

Mr. Sandman

The twisting hallways were decked with the personal belongings of people. He had to be careful while moving through the narrow space to avoid breaking things. He could tell they weren't just antiques because there were letters and trinkets and family portraits there. The dust would have normally triggered an attack, but for some reason he felt fine. This was the third room he had walked through? The fourth? He couldn't remember. He opened the door and stepped into the next room. A break in the pattern. The room was filled with broken hourglasses. The sand was frozen halfway. He moved through the twisting rows, bronze, silver, iron, gold all sorts of materials and wear. Small plastic egg timers and old nautical ones. Some with wings and others without. He spun a few around, but the sand refused to budge.

He was about to leave the room when he spotted a smallish one with green sand. It looked different, newer somehow. As he picked it up the glass began to spin violently in his hands. Before his eyes, centuries unfolded and the room and everything in it turned to dust, taken away to nothingness by a strong wind.

The space of the virtual

Professor at the University took own life

In a new blow to the govt.'s UNI program, a professor of philosophy and theory was found dead in their rooms this Monday. Professor Surf, was found unresponsive by his colleague Professor Turf when the latter went to pick him up for their morning lecture. According to initial reports he was found hanging from the rafters. Allegedly, the professor had been petitioning the UNI for an extended mental health leave for several months, but stayed on because his requests were repeatedly denied.

The UNI is expected to put out an official statement today; Mr. Turf declined to comment.

The space of the real

Pavan looked at the ceiling and felt it would collapse on him any moment now. The water damage was extensive. He turned his head groggily and looked at the room around him. The blinds on the window were old and greyed and closed shut. The only source of light in the room was a yellow zero-watt in the other corner from where he was. The only source of sound was the hum of the old air conditioner on his left. He lay back down and sighed. What had he gotten himself into? He really disliked this about her. This is why things hadn't worked out between the two of them. Jump first, Ask questions later. He had a splitting headache.

The door to his room opened slightly. A narrow wedge of light made him cover his eyes. He struggled to sit up.

'Good, you're up. I really thought we'd have to go to a hospital.'

'Who the fuck says we shouldn't go to one right now.'

'That isn't really a wise move considering that there are people after us.'

'Anamika, why are you so calm, the fuck's wrong with you?'

'Calm down. This isn't the first time someone's been after me.'

'It isn't?' Pavan felt uneasy. What had she been up to in the last four years? 'So I take it, you're no longer chained to a desk.'

She smiled. 'Nope, not anymore. Not for a long time. This is my third project.'

'Who are these people? And what exactly have you brought upon me?'

'Well I don't know who the guy at my apartment was. Could've been sent by any of the parties that are involved, to be honest. No one's too keen for this to get out. Not the government, and certainly not the people who want to steal it from them.'

'What are you talking about?'

'I Pavan am talking about influence, and control. I am talking about manufacturing consent and disciplining the minds of the herd.'

'What like some neuro-toxin or something?'

'Where did you get that from, Batman? No. Media. Memes, from what I can tell.'

Pavan had to bite his lip to stop himself from snapping at her. 'Media already is a totalised form of control Anamika. All it takes is repetition and reinforcement. This is nothing new, certainly nothing worth killing over.'

'Pavan, the way these people talk to each other in their inter-departmental memos you'd think that the dash avatar was here, they see it as a second coming. It isn't about whether or not it works. It matters that these people think it works. And the other interested parties are clearly invested in the narrative to send in people to off us.'

'Off you. Not me.'

'Yes, well comrade that is just a matter of semantics now. Might as well play the Internationale because it is an US they are after now, and OUR lives are on the line.'

'I will help you figure out who is after us, but as soon as they are apprehended, you and I – we're done.'

'We've been done for nearly half a decade now. Not an issue for me.'

'Where are we anyway? What is this dump?'

'This dump is one of three places my newspaper rents to serve as operating places for sting ops or as safe houses when shit hits the fan, which it almost always does.' She reached inside her pocket and took out the pills. 'Here take these. They'll help.' He took them quietly without water. She was always grossed out by his ability to do that. She had to break up her meds into half and still needed plenty of water to force them down.

'What time is it?'

'A little after one.'

'I think I'm going to lie back down.'

'Take some rest, I'll put on the water for the cup ramen.'

The space of the dream

He was falling through the void, with a bright lattice of endless logic spreading out in every direction. His skin felt like it was on fire. It was a digital baptisation. He tried to make sense of the characters and the numbers as he fell, but each section whizzed by so fast that he couldn't even see all of it, much less begin to piece the discrete bits of data together in his mind. He reached out into the emptiness and tried to claw at the lattice, hoping to hold on to the network. The bright characters slipped through his fingers.

He closed his eyes and felt the white hotness of the symbols pressed into his skin like a brand as they passed through him.

The space of the real

Anamika reached over and ruffled his hair. His eyes were closed and he looked peaceful. She felt a lump of sadness make its way to her throat. They had spent countless nights like this, in strange rooms, she could almost pretend this was one of them. The antique AC was trying its best to cool the room. She felt around for the bump. It had swelled up badly. She felt a little guilty. But there was no going back. She would get the paper to rush the piece so that Pavan could go back to his life. Back to his dusty room. He liked to pretend that he had left her, but she knew she had ended things.

He spent most of his time writing or rather worrying about writing. Hours and hours of worrying but none spent writing. Days and weeks of isolation spent doing anything and everything in the name of writing, but no actual work. She had finally tired of his endless 'me' time and walked out – just an endless parade of self-pity and grieving as a cover for selfish focus on himself. He had started working as a translator even before they had met. Maybe he already knew. She had watched the convolutions and the heteronyms get out of hand. The perils of genius. He did look cute in this lighting though. She rubbed his eyebrows out of habit and could feel the new wrinkles on his forehead. She could tell the last few years hadn't been a cakewalk for him. They hadn't been good for her either. She did have her career at least. Being here depressed her a little, a string of short fire and pops that fizzled out after this guy. And him, just all insecure about her actually being able to string sentences of her own together even if they were "just non-fiction that didn't even need any imagination." She sighed in the dark, and released her grip on his hair. She had gone from running her hand through them to pulling them out. Maybe she was holding on to some things. She couldn't fall asleep. How mad would he be with her if she put on a sitcom. She could feel the tiredness seeping through her body. But the adrenaline was keeping her up. Men always fell asleep easily. Sometimes it felt like all they did was come and pass out.

The ceiling in this place was really coming apart. She sipped on her coffee. It had gone cold. She hated it. They'd left her place all messed up. A part of her wanted to go there right now and tidy up a little. Maybe get some books, and her coffee. The stale smell of the coffee was covering up some of the staleness of the room. Anamika would have given anything to just be at her window at this time of the night. She never tired of it. The flowers in the street looked very sad in the moonlight. She let out a sigh. He was here next to her. In her bed after all these years. And the only thing she wanted was to be away and to be by herself. She had gotten used to him not being around and did not want to turn her back on all the time and the work it had taken her to get here.

She should not have used his pseudonym. Why did she? Why is that the first thing that came to her? A million names she could have made up. What a fucking cliché. She had asked her neighbour to close up her place. Thankfully she had called the police and they had the guy in custody. She was holding off on telling Pavan because she knew he would go straight back into his rabbit hole of a room. She wanted to make sure things were safe for him before he went back. Not something she needed on her conscience. Like enough hadn't been fucked up already. She wondered if some part of her wanted to see him again, but she had no desire to pull on that thread tonight. She had to stay focused. First thing tomorrow she'd have to look into the accounts of the guy who had attacked them. Once she traced who'd paid him, she'd have the final piece of the puzzle. She knew there wouldn't be much change, but all she could do was take a deep breath, work the sources and hope for the best. All her seniors were jaded by now. Maybe she was too, a little. There's only so much you can do, considering the way everything was.

No. Stop. She shook her head. She was second-guessing herself. She always did this to herself when he was around. It had been years since she'd felt this way. Even asleep he managed to be annoying. She slowly got up and made her way across the room to her bag and fished out her headphones. She scrolled through her playlists but ended up putting on some Lofi. She was less interested in music now. Most of the time all she had the energy for where atmospheric background noises. The stress of the day was finally beginning to catch up with her. She slipped into the covers and closed her eyes. She'd fix everything tomorrow.

The space of the symbolic

Ghost Story

She could feel the metallic coldness of the whistle all around her. It must be snowing outside. She turned around and put her hands against the silver. She raised herself on her toes and looked at her apartment through the tiny opening in the whistle. There was no one in the living room. She sat down dejectedly, curling up into a small bundle of herself.

She was back here – she didn't need to see the place to know how everything was outside her prison. Her apartment was still there in the Circle of Two. Her portrait was still hanging next to the whistle. On the mantle, idle letters were scattered next to volumes of Andrić, Sekulić, Dostoevsky and several biographies of Tesla. The girl who was living there now – she could see her reading by the window sometimes. The Tesla books weren't hers; they were her boy's and lately, he had been leaving more and more of his things behind.

She and the girl had both observed the changing tapestry of

their apartment. After her death, she had been extremely amused to find her spirit still persisting on the material plane. Her excitement was frightfully short-lived for she had soon discovered that she could not leave the boundaries of her old whistle. A lover had given it to her when they were marching in the streets against someone or the other. The country was rife with violence in those days – cigar and oil smugglers peppered the streets, walking furtively in long coats with raised collars.

He was warm. She felt safer when she was with him. He had died some years before her. The metal was cold. She would drift in and out of existence inside the whistle for a few hours and then stop existing – or at least she wasn't conscious for days, weeks, months – what is death if not a slow forgetting. Every time she came back to herself, she felt there was a little less of her left. Memories had vanished; there were entire years that were missing.

Many women had lived in her place after she had died. The girl was the fourth or the fifth. None of them had disturbed the whistle or her portrait. She let her mind drift off to the river that flowed as long as a year whose name she could no longer remember. Fragments of her years spent standing in the studio floated in and out of her. Supervising the camera angles on some show – overseeing the costumes for another – she had done all she could but things were back to the same place now.

'Why did you go without me?' She raised herself and peeked in out from the opening. They were arguing in the living room.

'You were away, a friend asked me to go and I agreed.'

'Hmmm'

The girl was looking out the window pensively. He tapped her lightly on her shoulder

'Let's go now?' The look on her face softened.

'But I don't have a whistle'

'It's okay. I am sure they must be selling some there at the protest.'

The girl nodded her head. She looked out of her prison in despair.

'Hey wait!' he pointed his finger straight at her – or rather at the photo on the wall. The girl smiled at him.

'It's like we are taking her with us' She raised herself on her toes and looked out of the little opening. The streets were overflowing with people. Old slogans were painted and raised on banners again. Svetlana suddenly realised that the metal was warmer now; the warmth from the girl's chest had permeated her prison. She felt the air change around her as the girl blew loudly on the whistle – she glided over the sea of protesters for a few moments before finally vanishing into nothingness.

The space of the virtual

Ajgar Sting Ops. Signal Chat

Nirava

We have received word from Anamika that the timeline for the D.O.M.A. piece has been accelerated. The overtime alone is going to be a headache. I need you all to clear the next few weeks. How long will you need to write it, Aruni?

Aruni

I can do it in five days, but you'll need to proof it as I go.

Vahini

Why the accelerated timeline?

Nirava

She was attacked in the afternoon today.

Nyra

Again?

Nirava

Yes. We'll be chasing leads on this tomorrow. We need to move on this and quick before someone else butchers the story. Would be four months of work down the drain. Any updates on the graphics?

Vahini

I haven't started on them, but I will tomorrow.

Nyra

Where was she attacked?

Nirava

Her flat.

Aruni

Then where is she now?

Nirava

That's on a need to know basis for now. I will keep you guys updated as and when she updates me on the situation.

The space of the real

Sub. #17

'And that's when I told her you know. You can fucking take It up the ass or I can take my business elsewhere. And then she looks at me with those big fucking eyes, and I cave you know. Next thing I know I'm going down on her and it's been an hour or two and I don't even know anymore. And my tongue boy, it's really fucked up at the point where it connects to the bottom of the mouth. And you know what she fucking tells me? She likes it slow. And that I'm being brutish and have been fucking up myself over something she doesn't even like.'

Q.

'What do you think I did, I got the fuck out of there. And then when I get home. I've been down on this big tit bitch for so long, that even three cigarettes and an espresso isn't enough to get her cunt smell out of my breath. And she smelled it on me as soon as I got close to her. But you know my wife, she never says anything. Not a fucking word. She gets these, whatdoyoucallit micro-expressions. And you can read her entire life story in that nanosecond. Who she's fucked, what her opinions on Descartes's

Meditations are, everything. And I just don't have the energy to push it anymore. So, I just went to bed. I don't even know if she slept in the same room that night.'

Q.

'The fuck I know. If I knew that I wouldn't be driving two hours out of my way to come to this shithole would I? I just opened the ledger for you. You tell me. You tell me.'

Q.

'No look I opened the floodgates on it right, I just went over to this different bitch the other day. And it's like they've started a committee or something. But you know she's much more open to things so I put it up her piping. But I'm still not happy.'

Q.

'WELL OF COURSE NOT.'

Q.

'Yeah so I went there. And I did that. But like she just refused to acknowledge it. Like the words were just floating through her and hitting the wall. And with every word I'm saying it's like another thing that is taking up space in that tiny room. But you know how I get; I can't stop once I've started. So, I keep going. And I keep going. And it's like this pattern that's repeating itself again and again. And we both know it so well now. And by the time I'm done it's like the room is filled with these things and I'm drowning or maybe suffocating. Anyway, there's no space left in the room. And it's nothing to her. Cause she's passing through everything see. And it isn't an issue for her. And that just makes me madder.'

Q.

What about it?

Q.

Look I don't give a fuck about that. That was just a money thing, I feel fine. Some extra cash for the side. It's not easy keeping all these side hoes.

Q.

Well, what does it matter? I feel no different. Maybe a little on edge. But that would happen to anyone if you strapped them to a chair and spun them around like they were volunteering for the fucking astronaut program. But the dizziness went away. And the pay was good. Now can I tell you about this bitch who wanted to give it to me up the ass with a strap on or not?

Sub. #8

'I went there to find something to do with my time. I had to support the family, and quickly. And they were the only ones who were hiring people with my limited skill set. And it did go well, we coasted over. And then dad fixed his troubles at business, so on the whole I don't really regret anything. I mean I know, maybe if he'd fixed things a little sooner then I wouldn't have been drafted for the experiment. But you know, you can't think like that. You can't just look at things that way or you'd regret doing anything and not doing anything. It's just a way to imbue all your decisions with regret retroactively.'

Q.

'Not more than anyone else. It's just how I look at things. Someone has to take responsibility, it just ended up being me.'

Q.

'No. Eww. Why would you say that? Are you like one of those anti-feminist women? It isn't a violation if I chose it. I had a choice and I made it. That's disgusting that you could look at it like that. Aren't you people supposed to be more progressive, or well-adjusted to not think this kind of shit?'

Q.

'No, I didn't mean that. Not in that way.'

Q.

'Yes, I understand.'

Q.

'Yes, I'm not saying that. But on any given day as a woman, you are questioned on your choices, even you. And this isn't something that someone picked out for me, I went for it. And I picked it. And in the end, I am not being a fatalist here. But you know how there's a genetic component to addiction. So, I don't see it as being helpless you know. There are choices that lead you to where you are, and you exercise whatever little free will you have in the area and then just get where you get.'

Q.

'Not really. But everyone looks at something and sees behind things. And it is the thing that you see behind the first that ends up defining you. Every subsequent thing you see behind is coloured with that first discovery.'

Q.

'For me? I'm not sure. I try to look for it, and sometimes I think I've found it. And then I remember something else that I feel must have been more influential. And as a result, everything is changed. And that really scares the shit out of me.'

Sub. #11

'Oh no, I had her pegged from the beginning. I knew what kind of a girl she was and I knew what kind of a guy I was. And I wasn't looking for anything more meaningful than two such people could find with each other or were even capable of.'

Q.

'I mean, that's the disappointment. It did go exactly the way I wanted it to. Or at least the way I had seen it going. But you know it isn't until something has gone the way you think you wanted it to that you realise that you wanted it to go a different way. And so that's how it went.'

Q.

'No of course not. If I had noticed any change I would have told you about it doc. I opened it and then I closed it, and that was the end of it. I stepped outside of myself a little. And it went the way it did. Neither good nor really bad either. I made a connection. However brief it was. I looked in her eyes, I let go of as much of the other shit things that I carry behind my eyes and really looked at her. Giving her access to me and everything. And it wasn't good enough.'

Q.

'Lady can you just listen for a moment. God. I realise that this is paid for by them. But can you stop pushing me in that direction, I will answer all of your questions. I will fill out the fucking survey. I'll write a detailed report if that's what'd make you happy. Just listen to what I'm saying first.'

Q.

'No, nothing happened after that. We exchanged a look and both of us knew that that was it; the exchange of the transaction. And so I left. I could have left something behind or a number even. I didn't want to cling on to the hope of things. It's a cleaner break this way. Just clean and over.'

Q.

'No, I'm not. Not anymore than anyone else. Maybe a lot less than most people. The way they go on about it, makes me feel that I have it pretty good. Well easier, if not good per se. As things go. I don't like to dwell on it. The other day I was walking by this park. And there was this guy with a Pitbull. I wanted to go over and pet the dog, but I didn't. And anyway, it's a fucking Pitbull so maybe that was for the best. And I thought to myself maybe you don't really need anyone to be happy with things. And that somehow it'd be healthier for me to just leave this thought behind and to forge on. I'm not saying this as a volcel thing or some inane form of Buddhism. I'd still sleep with women whenever I can or need to, but just clinging on to this expectation of this something more is just killing me. Who even really understands this Buddhism thing really. Just a bunch of peeps injected into the modern-day workforce hooked on copium trying to numb themselves out. Vajrayana, Stoicism they'll take whatever they can get. So, I'm not holding on to any expectations in that direction. I tried it, it didn't work. And I can't say that I was sincerely ever part of the workforce that I'd need to cope with any trauma or stress or anything. So, it has to be the constant mound of disappointments in my personal life that keeps on building up little by little. But I guess that's what every year does to you. Eventually, you know.'

Q.

'A little. After a long time to be honest. Well not since . . . you know. It just centres me more than any other thing, and as a tool it is useful when things get well you know.'

Q.

'Inside and out. Just cleanses you. That whole experience, those weeks – they were just a sensory overload of sorts. And that is how I deal with overloads. And it has worked so far. So why fix it if it ain't broke.'

Q.

'Lady, If only. I am not into that lifestyle thing. I look for the simple way out. Mind you not the easy way out, but the simple way out. And that is all it is. No point in complicating it beyond what is necessary. And no point in looking for over simplistic ways that won't get you out of the mess that you're feeling. And this isn't some self-help bullshit. It's tried and tested by me. It works for me. If you asked me why or how it works, I couldn't answer that. But that is for you lot to figure out. All I know is that it does. And that is good enough for me.'

Q.

Touché.

Q.

If there is one, I wouldn't know anything about that. As I said, not interested in over-complications.

Q.

'Yeah, I saw them. I didn't care much for any of them. Some attractive women, sure. But you don't really want to be in the company of people who are that desperate you know. And worse who know you are that desperate. And I get that there must be a camaraderie thing there that might work for some people. But I know that I am not one of those people. So why bother. I wouldn't hesitate if it was any other place in the world. Hell, would probably be tying myself up into knots over them if I saw them in a bar or a café or even in the metro. But that's just it. I didn't. And circumstances have this way of pulling away the veil. And however beautiful the person might be, once the veil has been pulled off things, they can never be the same. And that's just too depressing for me. Even if it somehow worked out, this is what I'd be secretly thinking about 24/7.'

The space of the symbolic

A Letter to Slowboat

This letter begins in the deep dark of an unwritten Dostoevsky novel. There are Russians huddled up in a room, debating god, man, atheism, socialism, the local madman, and other things that usually find room in such a setting. I flick my cigarette and leave the men to their squabbles. The moonlit streets of the unnamed village are silent now. The occasional yawning cat moves slowly in front of the people still out at these hours, taking care to bless the walkers with poor luck. I see out of time and place as I turn a corner, Kierkegaard throwing lines to a couple of lovesick prostitutes. The scene shifts to a nameless Mediterranean port town. A silhouette moves across the brightly coloured walls. A dagger falls and the blood sprays out in a fine mist before vanishing in the dead of night. Or perhaps it is a Caribbean port town. In other news, the camera that was used by Benjamin to capture dialectical images was exposed to light, The film has been ruined now. Chet Baker adjusts his false teeth, selects an embouchure and starts playing a cool tune. The streets turn to neon, old Windows 95 style graphics start taking over the landscape. 'Oh No Pooh! That's not honey you're eating, That's v a p o r w a v e ' /musicplays. Neon palm trees melt into sludge, a ladle turns the bubbling cauldron. 'Why are the Wolves White?' the Samurai wonders to herself as she sheaths her katana. A hot red Cadillac passes her, the Travelling Jazz Salesman looks at her in his rear-view mirror, Looks back at his Vinyls and lets out a deep tired SIGH. KERSPLAT! The silverfish on the wall dead in one swift movement, the slipper returns back to its place on the right foot. The tiny ship in the glass bottle is frozen in its place in front of a rather dull volume of Plato's Selected Works. Out of all the volumes in my room penned by Lakshmi Nidhi Khare, 'Roop ke Nupur' has the best cover. It is an aged shade of blue that features a naiad on the cover with her feet on a lotus petal and a peacock feather in her hair. It is also the most dull in terms of its contents. The entire thing is one big love poem to his wife, who frankly from what I've seen of her in old yellowed photos, didn't warrant this voluminous a literary output. 'Jeevan ke Gaate Swar' has a shit cover, faded green with red text on it, at least the poems inside are nice. Is there central heating in Hell? In old stories in the Poetic Edda, Grimnir is wiser and Loki is duller than what they are today. Should I call the word Kafkaesque, If I cannot find a better word for it? What do Lovecraft's cat and Huckleberry's friend Jim have in common? One drag from this North Eastern (made in Delhi) clay pipe and your lungs won't stop burning. Why is the pipe empty? Hey! It isn't empty. Didn't you know the state has just legislated the existence of aether back into the physics textbooks. It is an established fact that Wittgenstein jacked off to Quadratic Equations at the war front. If someone had grafittied the solution to P/NP on the walls across from his windows, It wouldn't be conjectural to say then that he would have died instantly in a state of orgasmic bliss. I don't like to step inside the pages of anything De Sade has written without my shoes on. Who wants to slip in blood, semen and pussy juice? The sunglasses that I acquired in Goa are missing the lens on the left hand side. But I like them this way. The constructive and the destructive interference of the incoming light cancels out the world. The streets are empty now. I think the pandemic is here to stay. If Nietzsche was to fall down in fits outside right now, Would I break curfew to go hold his Hand? Winter cools indifferently the sidewalks of Beirut, of Delhi, of Chicago, Of your heart and Of mine. Spring is ending now, but the vines are covering my car more fearlessly everyday now that the Gardner's rusty shears aren't troubling them. In an empty comedy club, A stand up rolls back his sleeves, adjusts the mic at an angle to his mouth, and holds the mic stand with his other hand: 'What's the deal with Time?' Hey Hey, Come now, Why would you say something so brave yet so controversial? And why would you say something so widely accepted yet so boring? Everyday I have the Blues. 'Time and Space died . . . . Yesterday!' Well then, All I can say is: ' May you rest . . . . In Jazz'. The film you're about to see has been entirely handpainted by a team of over 100 artists. (moody pop song playing) Do not throw your cigarette butts on the ground. We've caught the dogs smoking and we're trying to get them to quit. The letter is a train ride now from one unknown Norwegian town to another. Korean Indie Pop plays softly in the background. The train weaves through modernist glass buildings and come onto pastoral greens, with clean blue lakes and soft morning blue skies that meet on the horizon on small hills. Come and have a dream in Technicolor with me. The lakes green now, and the tracks diverging and converging on intersections through the soft green landscape. Someone else is on here with me, Wouldn't it be fantastic to get off with her now and be lost under the sunlight. And my heart might melt like fire on ice, and the inner city lights would fall on her face, Wouldn't it be nice, But such a cliché . . . The train is going around the rim of a wine glass now a single mother is looking at the silent world outside through her window, the 4am wind soft on her face, and the stars shining on her glass. On the sidewalk an unused cigarette pack, The warning reads 'Death is the most certain possibility (M.Heidegger)' Knock Knock Knocking on Heaven's door. It's 2021, Jesus! Get a doorbell. If we all have to eat from the trashcan of ideology, then I pick the one behind the five star hotel for anorexics. They will call me, ... The Van Gogh of Memes. Why are the Kapibaras taking a yuzu hot bath? Because they want to be lemoney fresh. Kill you Darlings! But remember to cryo-preserve them, in case science becomes sufficiently advanced in the future. A monkey on a typewriter hitting keys at random for an infinite amount of time will almost surely (Probability = 1) type out any given text, such as the texts of William Shakespeare. How many more lines do I have to type before this text turns into Hamlet before returning back to Gibberish again? On my cup, A portrait of Portugal, In black and sepia. No matter how hard I squint at it, I can't see Pessoa's statue sitting outside his café. Bill Withers just died. Ain't no sunshine when he's gone. The baddest motherfucker to ever put on an orange turtleneck. Gone. Only Darkness everyday. Editing space and time is a bitch. Where is the Ant colony that I found living inside my Hermes 3000 when I got it? Oh that's right, they are dead. Modern problems require Modern solutions. Postmodern problems require Postmodern solutions. Postpostmodern problems require Postpostmodern solutions. In Fragments, Truth, Found, Lost in the spaces between the words. In March 1942, Cocteau wrote 'Tous les jours, je me disais : c'est inutile d'ecrire un journal maintenant. J'ai vecu plusieurs existences. Je n'ai pas ecrit'. I too have lived many lives that I never wrote down. And I still don't see the need to keep a

Journal even as his sit on my desk, smelling of old dank libraries and death. Lying down in a jail cell, On the floor Bob Kaufman poking a pen into the air trying to write words on the trapped winds. On the moon, would you rather watch an earthrise or an earthset? This world has little use for old poets, better to die young. Leave them wanting more, instead of overstaying your welcome. I think I am losing too many hair. Everyday I see them on the ground, I am more aware now because there isn't much to do all day. How long before I seize upon a pair of scissors and do the deed myself? Sun Wukong could summon clones by pulling out his hair, If I shared the monkey king's power how many of my clones die idly everyday? Why are cupcakes not eaten out of cups? In an old diner, somewhere in the backstreets of Tokyo a man looks despondently in the space hunched over a bowl of ramen. On the empty streets outside, Deer wander under the neon. How many Scandinavian metal bands are lost in the woods shooting album covers? Despair is not indifference. Even in despair there are things that are protected. Cool Bossa Novan sounds layered over the Latin Jazz arrangements by Cuban bands. Smith Corona Corsair Deluxe/ Made in England. Flick flick flick flick late 70s clean sound. I'm Russian, I romanticise things. In six months of waking up early in the cold, Descartes died. Unwise to give up habits formed over a lifetime for princesses. I do not attempt to capture impressions of nature. The poor poet rots in his room. And the room rots with him. Inconsequentially some things or somethings were dismissed out of hand. Each passing day adds to dread and to indifference. Time to play postrock beats to chill/ cry to. . . . . That I am here now and living this life has always felt surreal. Not because of any mystical or metaphysical reason, but because on some level it is unacceptable to me that my father is dead. It creates a layer of reality over the one that's here now, One where he is in fact alive, and all of this is a dream. Where does the dream begin? Where does the sky end? I feel a resting warmth on the bottom of my stomach as I write these things. Not a comfortable warmth. A wornout shoegaze track is playing in the background, an empty glass is resting next to me. The sand is all in the bottom of the hourglass, stuck, unmoving. Unmovable. It is easier to think now of all the ways in which I am disappointing the ones around me. Vintage Misery. If put in a podcast these sentences could at least get me some views. What songs did I fill my playlist with before I found the ones that are on there now? This letter finds itself lost in the everydayness of my life. There are too many hours and too little life to fill them with. How many connections to the old world have we lost. How many possible futures lost? We are haunted by our lost futures. *cue canned sitcom laughter* If Alice was here what youtube rabbit hole would she fall down? How big a leap is it to go from Kandinsky to Malevich? An inadvertent Jump-Cut due to removing excessive or unwanted film can be covered up by cutting to the close-up of a bystander. * cut away to close-up of bystander * And then she wrote to me 'sending virtual hugs', So naturally I had to write back 'Shall I send you a virtual stabbing' and then she . . . The bystander stops suddenly and breaks the fourth wall, Looking at the audience through the lens, and beyond them at the writer through the paper. This outline is subordinated to the stylized rhythm of Jazz. I had wisdom. In order to give proof of it, I sought to remember. To forge it into knowledge. , and in so doing, Lost it. Time is an Illusion. Only backpain is real. Coffin Dance but it's Jazz. Terror. A door opens in the narrative, a hand with blackened nails slowly turns the doors on its hinges that squeak out sending shivers through the sentences next to it in the text, An unshaven stranger looks around at the text, noting the events and the passage of time. He takes out a watch, turns the dial clockwise and anti-clockwise until he is satisfied with the results, after which he goes back to his place in the narrative which is the future.

They were at it again. Ever since Moksh had gone abroad, that's all his parents did with their time. They would have separated a long time ago if they were in some other country, but the co-dependence and their skittishness at being one of "those" people just made them stick with each other. It was just white noise to Vikram at this point. He had the submission deadline coming up for a short film festival and on Daris's and Karna's insistence had decided to complete and submit his film. The edit was coming along nicely. He had a friend doing some of the sound edits, and if he just kept his head down, he knew he'd make the deadline. He wasn't completely happy with the industrial music he had to sub in since he couldn't find a CRT player worth a damn.

The yelling was getting louder now. He looked at his door. They were still in their room. He got up and closed it off before they had a chance of dragging him into their shit. When his brother was here at least some of it got diluted between the two of them but now without him here, Vikram got the worst of it. Nothing is more disappointing than to be caught in the pattern of someone else's life.

Vikram leaned back in his chair and rubbed his eyes. What would Neha be doing now? Probably some hot girl shit. He wanted to text her but decided it would be best if he didn't. Karna had been looking into the department already and had some idea of what exactly the volunteer project was that Neha had been a part of. The way these things pervaded the fabric of things saddened him. Just the constant normalisation of letting yourself be used as a lab rat for money, and if you weren't that desperate and did everything right – then just ending up on the hamster wheel of endless mundane work. He wanted to make something. A film that would change things. But he had grown up watching them – Films that when you watched them made you feel that they could change the world. And in the decades since they had come out, nothing had changed. Maybe even worsened on some fronts. Things just keep on spiralling – in his house, in his life, in the world. New catastrophes and just a world limping through every day. People just keep looking for people who are screwed up in ways that somehow fit in around the edges of our lives. Everything just dissolved into vanity with him. The greats before him were sculpting in time, capturing light on celluloid, thinking great big thoughts and all he could do was compulsively obsess with the minutiae of his own life.

He looked at the frame he was working on. Every frame a painting, right? All he could do right now was finish this short before the deadline. And then hope for the best.

The space of the symbolic

Comprehension

03. Keeping true to Euclid's Lemma there is an 'a' who is an angsty teenager who has discovered existentialism and is now throwing their life away pouring over endless hours of continental philosophy that will for a while continue to give them insight into themselves and into the nature of the world around them. 'a' has read every text out there and has exhausted the general vistas of Philosophical Enquiry and now reads particular and niche texts hoping to replicate the initial rush of discovery which is now impossible because everything is a repetition or a recycling of something they are already familiar with or have intuitively derived on their own from what they've read. Show that every positive odd angsty teenager 'a' is of the form as $a = Xq + r$ where q is some philosopher.

05. The transvaluation of all values that leads to something more honest than the empty pendulous movements of the dialectic that transmutes and creates dangerously a new way of evaluation itself. The categories of hollow alienation were obliterated and erased from the plane on which the previous ways of feeling were charted out.

08. It bears to remember that the convergence of the function that results in the Mandelbrot set proved to be connected topologically; the conjecture of whose local connectivity is still an open problem. For the iterations of $f(x) = x2 + c$ that do not escape to infinity for the complex values of 'c' where 'x' takes on the values of thoughts that curve in on themselves in endless complexity and fractals of thoughts go into themselves and magnified and isolated and magnified and isolated until the beginning s of the fractal are almost entirely forgotten. Find solutions that bring you back to the first iteration.

13. The exteriority of writing is like some object that is at hand and induces pathological mistakes in people that are then gleefully mapped by the peddlers of linguistic models.

17. The value of the project of enlightenment is not limited to the action of world-making. It is equally critical to the task of making the self. The image of a 'Human' carving themselves out of a stone block is concomitant with Prometheanism. The push against Prometheanism based on its 'proactive violence' is made from positions that allow for the systemic violence to exist as long as it can be theorised into 'small pockets of resistance.' The 'missing people' cannot be found and the 'subaltern cannot speak,' but the missing people never lost themselves and the subaltern never stopped speaking. The attack on the 'hubris' of Prometheanism is an attack first and foremost on the ability of the 'Human' to dominate domination and having done so, to abolish it.

The space of the dream

The High-rise

It happened three different times. They weren't around for the first one or the last one. On the second time, they saw the dismantled houses put together into piles of bricks – red kiln – grey cement bricks.

The salvageable tin was stacked neatly in a corner, and the rusted segments were scattered around in the empty area where their houses once stood. Some of them had Om or Crucifixes drawn on the tin in Chalk. Various personal belongings that the labourers had failed to collect were mixed in with the rubble. Of the jhuggis that were still standing, three had satellite TV dishes on them. Half of them were deserted now.

The kids were playing around with the water hose the next day when they saw the bricks being carted off in the direction of the final tower.

The Jhuggis

On their last days in the Jhuggis, when they were set to return to their own villages, the kids wanted to do something to commemorate the event. Mayank looked all over the place for Hassan, but couldn't find him anywhere. He had no interest in hanging out with the others. And he had no interest in crackers.

He walked the length of the settlement, and finally decided to risk knocking on his door to see if he was in. He disliked Hassan's Ammi and had no desire to see her face this early in the morning. But this might be their last day and he wanted to hang out with him before he left. The cement felt hot under his feet as he knocked on the tin. Someone growled at him from inside. He knocked again. A man opened the door. It wasn't Hassan's Abba.

'What do you want?'

The bricks from their jhuggis were used to finish the tower and even though they never came to know of this, the ones from the third and final deconstruction found their way to the corner temple that some of the residents had previously requested be built.

The empty space left after uprooting the jhuggis was turned into a garden.

*

She looked at the warehouses that dominated the entirety of her view and sighed to herself.

The sun had almost dipped below the horizon. She turned her head and looked at the ugly clump of high-rises in the far-off distance. This wasn't the landscape she wanted to look at every day. But it would have to do for now.

'What do you want to do for take-out?'

'Oh, you pick. I'll pick next time.' He was trying to get the streaming up and running.

Mayank felt nervous as the man towered over him. He stank of alcohol, and his eyes were yellow with red veins in them.

'Hassan', he murmured.

'Hunh?'

'Hassan', He said again, making the timbre of his voice deeper.

'There's no Hassan Wassan here', the man growled at him. Mayank looked him squarely in the face. He turned around and walked away. He walked around in the scorching heat asking people if anyone knew where he was.

Finally, someone told him to go look for Amit in the last building.

He had to wait for the construction elevator to be loaded up with the grouting material before he could finally ride it all the way to the eighteenth floor. The lift started moving precariously up the shaft with the gears creaking with the strain. He felt his heart tighten up a little

'I'm just going down for a bit.'

He nodded and went back to his work. The rent was cheap. It was cheap. It was cheap. It was cheap.

That is the only thing she could say to feel marginally better about things. She felt more lost now than ever. Shouldn't things be simpler now? So many things were out of the way. Work was sorted. So was home and travel and food and love.

The stairs looked a little uneven on some floors. On others, they were perfectly made. Why was she noticing all of this only now?

She was becoming more and more lost again. Her hopes and dreams and all those little details were where she wanted them to be, maybe it will take some more time for them to settle down.

She looked at the neat clean shrubbery that lined the garden as she walked around the path. The entry gate was also crooked.

as he looked at the settlement down below. The dismantled shanties looked dismal from this height. The ones on the edge which had only been partially dismantled, reminded him of the photo of the ruins that their teacher had shown them in a picture book in school last year.

The men standing next to him were leaning heavily against the walls. One of them was leaning against the door of the lift. Mayank wondered if he should say something. But he didn't want to be yelled at again, and so he decided to keep mum. As they stopped, the small wall of the elevator dropped and landed on the building. He waited for every-one else to get off before he carefully made his way to the floor. He was on the twentieth floor.

He was secretly happy to be leaving this place. The room they lived in was cramped and small and the tin overheat-ed in the summer months.He didn't understand why they had to come and live here when they had a big house in

Why hadn't she paid attention to all these details when they'd come in here the first time around?

The garden was lined with statues of Buddha, with a larger one dominating the centre. Some of them had lights under them, some didn't.

As she looked at his face, smiling in stone, all she could think about was running away from the place and never coming back again.

*

He had left again for the weekend.She was playing around with her food as she waited for the meeting to be over. Lately, she had been working from home more often. She liked staying in her bed and making her lunch every day, but the meetings and calls felt interminable. The house had grown softer around her as she had filled the corners with her things. His things were also there. They felt alien and strange. She felt like they were staring at her in his absence.

the village and farms and even schools with cool rivers and trees and shade. He dodged a man carrying a cement bag on his back and skipped around the welder fixing the staircase railing.

Even if he didn't find Hassan, it would be okay. He would be on his way back home tomorrow all the same.

He had to look inside all the flats on the floor before he finally found Amit lying down on the floor watching something with his brother on the phone. Their sister was lying asleep next to them.

'Eey, have you seen Hassan?'

Amit turned his eyes lazily away from the screen and looked at him.

'What?'

'Hassan, do you know where he is?'

'He left.'

Mayank felt a little sad at this, but it was to be expected.

She missed her rooms. Her home and the flat she had rented before this. Those rooms had been filled with her things, with her.

Sometimes there was not much in them except for a mattress on the floor and some books, but she felt they were warmer than this place.

She got up and decided to make some coffee. She looked at his French press as she poured in her instant coffee in the pan. The frothy bubbles spinning around inside looked like a sad lonely galaxy to her.

As the water started to boil on the edges of the pan, the galaxy was pulled apart and vanished. She quietly poured it in her cup and added the milk.

The cacti on her balcony had died.

Where else would he be if his parents weren't in the shanty.

'Any idea why they left?'

'Don't you listen to the news?' Mayank was irritated at this. Just because Amit's father had given him his old phone, Amit had started behaving as if he was entirely different from them. What business did he have keeping up with the news.

'His family fled in the night. '

'Fled?'

'Because of all the lafda in the capital.'

'Hmm.' He thanked Amit and started making his way back to his mother. Mayank thought about Hassan looking at the fields and the cities passing by his window as he rode the train back home.

The space of the real

As he looked around the room, he couldn't help but feel a little disappointed. He knew most of the key people wouldn't expose themselves like this in public. But from what he could see of the people sitting in the corner of the café, none of them appeared to have any authority or importance.

It was to be expected from a group of people who spent most of their time on /theory/ and /pol/ boards. And from what he could see, none of them were incels or theorycels. The presence of the three women at the table gave the group some credibility. More than what was owed to them in his opinion. Karna walked over to them slowly, and as soon as he got within earshot, he was hit by a barrage of online jargon that sounded awkward irl. People were introducing themselves using their usernames or tags. Two or three of the core members looked more settled and weren't as over eager as the first time attendees.

This was it: the accelerationists. He had decided before hand to go in as a first timer and not mention any of the texts he was in possession of. Or what he knew about them looking into the research that D.O.M.A. was doing. He knew he'd learn more by listening. He walked up and casually introduced himself using his username. One of the girls spoke up and gave him her own. He recognised it.

So, she was the one who had extended him the invite. Properly speaking, he had no business being here. He hadn't mentioned his blog or work to anyone online and as such had no standing amongst them. He had given hope of learning more about what they were up to owing to their suspicion of outsiders. That was until one over eager username had contacted him and offered an exchange. He had brought the fragments of the Parsani papers that he had with him.

'Uh, we don't use our real names here. So please refer to your username or just give some other name that you would like the others to use.' Karna looked at the corner. It was one of the older members. He was on his phone and hadn't looked up while speaking. Karna noticed how absorbed the guy was in his role as the 'knowing elder of the guild' and simply nodded in acknowledgment.

Karna pulled a chair and prepared himself for a long evening.

The space of the dream

As the men made their way across the endless barren that the world had now become, one looked to the other and said:

The last two left now
Only seeing the other
Fearing the cold wind
Beneath the empty branches
Our shadows move together

His companion considered for a moment and replied:

There is still more warmth
Looking at another's shade
Than to be alone
Left to stroll the white garden
For aught but to walk circles

Although the first man wasn't satisfied, he decided not to say anything to the contrary. Seeing his companion's silence, the first man said:

There in snow country
That volcano stands alone

Fuming ash and smoke
How lonely is the mount now
Look to him, See solitude

The first man weighed his companion's words and looked ahead at the peak that was issuing smoke, the ash and the snow indistinguishable to his old eyes. He felt the wind pushing him forward with its cold fingers and unthinking said:

To be free from want
The solace of not being
At the horizon
Senseless to reach for a hand
As transient as this cold wind

The space of the symbolic

Consider the simulation. Consider the flying symbols that stitch together to form the veil that overlaps a vacuity and becomes what you see and experience around yourself as the world. Consider the spectacle played out cyclically on this phantasmal theatre stage. Consider the synaptic fires of pure ecstasy refreshed at every two second interval. Consider the black ink on page and electron fires on cathode tubes. Consider the alignment of the liquid crystals and the organic diodes. Consider the conic ocular interactions with photons reflected from the green of cellulose and the diffracted blue of the aerosphere. Consider the binary fuel that switches this simulation from one state to the other. Consider the vibrations that spell it out for you. Consider the passing through of all this and more through the in between spaces that form you. Now blink.

The space of the real

All of a sudden, he felt himself waking up from a dream of falling. He had a fear of heights and hated these dreams. Anamika was on the bed next to him. Without thinking he reached out for her. His hands found the small of her back. She turned to him. She couldn't sleep either. Pavan felt around for her hand and took it into his. He felt like she was seeing through him with her eyes. Slowly he braved the waters and started to pull her to him.

She locked her lips with his and bit into them, softly at first but harder to the point where he felt the blood in his mouth. He reached out for her other hand and pinned her down. Their hands were moving around each other's bodies. She pulled down his pants expertly with her toes as he struggled around with the buttons on her shirt. He tried to force her down again but suddenly she was on top of him.

He felt himself falling into her.

The space of the symbolic

You open your eyes and see the grey sky from the little cracks in between the curtains. It's hard to know if it is the crack of dawn or if it's going to rain. As you try and rub out the sleep from your eyes trying to see if any alarm is going to go off, the notifications from the last few hours have already piled up. You make your way through them, dismissing the spam and replying to the urgent messages – none of them are urgent but you reply to some of them all the same. You were up last night, thinking. You were supposed to be up last night working, but nothing came to you and so for hours on end you stared at the glow of the feed while something played on the laptop and before you had realised the light had already gone off and the only sound in the room was that of the fan and the occasional barking dog. Now that you're up with that bad taste in your mouth the only thing that you want to confirm is that you've not missed the log in time at your work from home job. You have never met half the people you are working with, and you like it better this way. People come into your department, you teach them the basics and then they're sent into the circulation. You open your phone to play some music and get an ad for ulcer medication instead. You wait the customary five seconds before hitting skip and then hitting skip on the second ad before you finally get to your indie pop ballad or Lofi morning mix that helps ease you back into conscious existence. You shouldn't be getting an ad but you forgot to renew the subscription and for some reason the amount of work needed to get it back to the way it was seems insurmountably greater than letting the ads play on and on. There is some of last night's coffee left over in the cup next to you, but you don't drink it because you're not sixteen anymore and not trying to imitate every depresso mcexistential loner you've been reading or watching this week. It would be nice if someone could bring you some coffee in bed, but you know that ain't happening. So you decide to let a track or two play out before you get to it yourself. Among the confusing jumble of things inside your head there is an unfamiliar thought that you don't recognise the source of. You get out of bed and get up. You have the same feeling that you get when you move through a door or enter a new room exiting another having lost the reason for the exiting and the entering. There's nothing new about the idea, it's plebeian. You would have stopped thinking about it if only you could make sure what the genesis of the idea was. It feels a little out of nowhere but there's no point in dwelling on it now that it is here. The only way out is to trick yourself into doing something else and hope that what you want to know will come to you because you're not looking for it. And if it doesn't well then you're already doing something else. The newspaper is here with a big flap ad. You really need to cancel the subscription. Everyone else seems to be asleep. It is morning but on a Sunday. There are grey clouds out there but no rain. You sit down with your first cup. You've over done it. You should've paid more attention to the heat on the stove, instead of being lost inside your own head. No one needs to spend this much time thinking. There is something inside your head about that thing you saw in the news section on the edge of the fold of the paper. Or is it from something you saw on the data feed or something someone sent to you last week. There's nothing concrete about any of it but some of it lingers. And makes itself feel more imminent than the furniture you're sitting on. You are waiting for things to break out of this cycle but the waiting itself is something that comes and goes. Everywhere from the start of this and to the end of time you look at yourself in the mirror and convince yourself that all you need to do is make it through the next few days. But this isn't the first 'next few days' and you know that going forward you'll have more 'next few days.' You know the things you need to tell yourself in order to make it through these spells. It took you some years to figure this out but now you know. It's more or less the same every time and even if it isn't, you have managed to figure out ways of navigating through the swamp. You haven't been out in a while. You see people out on the street all the time, but the truth is you have no desire to be out there. Maybe something will hit you in a few days and suddenly you'll find yourself in the company of friends who are conveniently near at that moment. But not today. Today is just like any other day, you log in and then go through the motions. You play some music in the background or stream something on a borrowed subscription to a service that still has something you haven't seen. And you know you'll make it through. Somehow.

The space of the real

She could see the Chief talking to the liaisons outside the lab door. Navya rearranged the charts and the statistics she had the assistants prep for the visit today. It wasn't a courtesy call. They were here to either increase the funding or to gut their budget. The Chief had assured everyone that they'd all be safe. She wasn't worried about her place here. But it'd be hard to lose one of her underlings. The new guy, maybe not so much. But he had fixed the espresso machine the other day.

The main reason various attaches and liaisons showed up to their department or any department was mainly to fill their time and to create the appearance of work. They could have left the budget be, but then where would be the all caps CHANGE that the ruling majority had promised this term.

The Chief looked pleased with himself. A little too much for her taste. She was going to enjoy watching him out on his ass when she took over the Department ahead of his schedule. The liaisons shook his hand and left. That was unusual. In her experience they postured, and pressed buttons both on machines and people. While racking their brains for some fact or titbit that they could then insert into the conversation as they waited for the people who did the actual work to acknowledge their intelligence.

The Chief was still standing in the hallway. She decided not to go to him and waited for him to come to her. She could see him in the doorway, leaning against it. The man rarely looked that dejected. Not good news then.

'They gut the budget?' She decided to break the silence.

'Gut us? They fucked us over. Fucked us in our asses with a rusty iron rod.'

Navya pushed the charts away and looked at the man. 'If it's not the budget. What then?'

'They're going to bring in Credence to run the department. They'll send over the details of the transition in the next few months. They won't get rid of you. Or anyone who knows anything about what really happens in this facility.'

'They might as well have. You know what Credence does to R&D departments.' Navya said coolly. She racked her brain trying to think of ways out of this shit storm. But the man went on. 'All of this. This work. Your research, and more importantly my work. The book I've been working on. None of it will ever see the light of day. The fine print. The fucking thin fine line they used to fuck us over with. Credence wants to use this on their own users first. And the PM is in their pocket, so it's already signed and stamped. We're fucked. Get that through your fucking head.'

Navya looked at his face. Spittle had been flying out of his mouth and was getting all over her morning reports. The nerve on his forehead was bulging, to the point where it felt it might burst, killing him on the spot. She had never fully appreciated how ugly the man was.

The space of the symbolic

An absent 'A'

Forgetfulness is by now instinctive to her. Sometimes when she moves through her home, idle thoughts slip through her into the concrete below, never to be found or seen. Her thoughts unthinkingly follow those lines of flight which pierced through the known modes of remembering. When in the hold of ennui she tried to hold on to those bright slivers drifting off into the endless forgetting. Their lostness confirmed to her once more.

Epistemically effacing 'E'

At midnight his mind an unwitting victim of sorrow, anguish, misgivings, wrath and occasionally jouska. Thoughts zigzagging through his mind, swiftfoot unthinking moving through asphalt highways of his mind. Words that mark out horizons of vanity and vacuity. Words that build forts of signs and grammar at play on voids that signal a futuristic crisis – Signifying Nothing.

'I' interred in infinity indefinitely

They looked at the face reflected back at them. Unable to see beyond what was there placed near them, reluctant to reach out for flesh and blood that wasn't them. Always stretched out over the endless fractal of the temporal real but never the perceptual here. Someday they'd conquer the vastness that lay at the nucleus of the soul. And then blood and marrow will be sewn back together as one around the core that would no longer refuse.

Orienting 'O' onto Oblivion

What is that but a nameless thing that lies there. What advantage is there in this thing that is but hasn't any isness. Tidy cities and rivers all neatly arranged and pressed at the mapmaker's table – waiting in the space between spaces; unblemished. The measurer sees the inked parchment in amazement – staring at the patch where his hand impressed the nullity.

Unseeing 'U'

The invasion of the ontological was imminent. There was little that was to be done to stave it off. The ocean bed had been explored and endless mines of meaning had been emptied in the search of the panacea – the miners came back empty handed, having lost their memories to the canaries inside.

The space of the dream

The train platform was in the middle of an endless ocean of still water. The tracks ran a little under the surface in front of the little platform before disappearing off into the distance on both ends.

No train ever came.

She never lifted her head to check for one. There was no one else here with her nor would there ever be. She would sometimes look to the horizon hoping for a great big ship. But never a train.

The weather changed. So did the seasons. The colour of the water changed from the early deep red sky to cloudy light blues to dusk embers and then midnight starry blue.

The wind was a relief. It carried away her bitterness and her exhaustion. Sometimes it rained. The shed over the platform protected her. She liked the sound of rain striking against the metal. The ocean drank in the countless droplets – not a single ripple on its surface.

The space of the real

'And that's how it goes.'

'Round and Round.'

'Round and Round.'

They were sitting opposite the large imposing façade of the Department of Memetic Archaeology. The marble of the bench was chilling him to his bones. Winters in Delhi were Vikram's favourite part about living in the city. The dim lights of the buildings illuminated their surroundings a little before dispersing into the fog. Her shoulder was touching his. He wondered how long it had been since he'd last been out with a girl on a night like this. They had decided to ditch the recorders for tonight. When you start looking at everything as a part of something to put inside of a frame, a lot ends up being left out. Neha had just finished telling him about her time in D.O.M.A. Her nose was red from the cold. He wanted to say something that would make her feel warm but nothing came to him.

'There's really no point to it.'

'You could always do it for the others.'

'Charity for nameless and faceless people doesn't get you anything. It's nice to think like that, but it leaves you with nothing. Not even the satisfaction of seeing anything change. You wait long enough, and every little thing that you tried to better, ultimately ends up making something or the other worse.'

Sometimes she reminded him of one of those sad women from a Rohmer or a Godard feature. She didn't dress in the same pale muted colours, but she always managed to underscore her outfit with a jacket or a scarf that had a sombreness about it that Vikram had only ever found in obscure and unusable words.

'One of my friends is having this thing next week. She's very OCD about knowing who exactly will be there. I was thinking maybe you'd want to come?'

'I'd love to.' Vikram wanted to reach out for her hand but she'd put her hands inside her sleeves.

'You know, sometimes it isn't even bad. Evenings like these. Quiet. Cold but warm.' She shifted a little closer to him. 'I sometimes have these dreams where I think I'm in the real world, and everything is good and somehow all the disappointments of my life have never happened. A part of me remembers and knows what the real is and how this dream that I'm in isn't, but somehow it feels like the time I'm in then is somehow the future and everything that went wrong has somehow been fixed. But you know, just that sliver of recall of what did go wrong fills me with a deep dread whenever I look at the nice and good things in the dream. Everything feels like it would shatter again, the same way it already did. It keeps building up until I can't take it anymore, and then I wake up in these cold sweats in my bed.'

She sighed out into the cold, the cloud of her breath lingered briefly in the air before it vanished. 'You know, I think I'm almost relieved when I wake up and know the worst has already happened. I would take that any day over having everything back but living with the fear that they'll be taken away again.'

Vikram looked at the starless sky above him and closed his eyes, and breathed in the night air.

XLR8

The Knight's Tour of Hyperstitional Chmess
Thursday November 3rd 2027
Categories: Chameleons and Conspiracies

It isn't lost on anyone that the future is entirely lost to us or has been abducted and is being held hostage in an unreachable space. The onrush and onslaught of seemingly radical ideas whizzing past us as we stand still and unmoving offers little consolation or hope for what is to come. There is a proactive desire to retroactively build a soft aesthetic past that never existed and inhabit pockets of time that open in between the mind- numbing haze of the cybernetic present. Now you know, I've tried to platform Left Wing Accs. on this blog over any other head on the Hydra. I have spent the last few years looking for Hyperstitions in the texts of obscure and uncertain men, and while I have learned a lot from the texts. A part of me wonders if my time wouldn't be better utilised in distilling what I have formulated and enacting it into praxis. I don't want to admit it, but perhaps the waters are too muddied now that certain things have come to light. The ease with which the sands shift in Acc. Circles, and the marginal ideashifts that move the knight from one position to another are cause for concern. A part of me didn't want to admit this, perhaps because of the speed of the quick and complicated moves I never noticed what I thought was speed, was constrained by the squares of the board. And even if every inch could be travelled, the return to the same start position became inevitable after a certain number of moves. The need for a sociotechnical hegemony remains unchanged, but it won't come from any exchange of ideas that has room for disruption and needless tangentiation. The process modes that can enable gradients of a new post-capitalist thought will need to be based on a solid footing, a footing that needs more consideration and pause than I have given myself in the upkeep of this digispace in the last seven years. With this, I am not advocating a move towards the cynical endless-dialetithink or the neo-liberal's self-contentment drive but for perhaps a slower and careful build of engines from existing thought that can move the system to better ends, faster.

I am not going to give up on this space. But you will notice a longer gap between posts. And maybe a curvilinear shift towards better forms of the ideas that have been a staple of this website.

The space of the symbolic

So when you think of Kierkegaard on the corner of some street in Delhi, throwing out lines to lovesick women going about their business, I would tell you about Nietzsche dying in some street next to the ghoda gaadi; and you have to know it isn't one of those well-bred mares that I'd be on about, but the feedbag strapped white and sickly thin ones with the Band Baja banner on the back; and your mind would immediately go to the black gondola on the black gutter bearing Wagner across, which would immediately make me think of the women who would fall over themselves on seeing Lizst who fell down a stairway to his death, which would then take you to Schopenhauer pushing his mother off a staircase, and I might then think of dead mothers and crashes that would lead to Camus' wrecked car on the DND expressway, which leads to the unimaginative streets of suburbia walked by Kant in the evenings, which would make you remember cooler evenings in the Himalayas where on his way to his morning lessons Descartes' lungs are ticking to the hour of his demise, which would remind me that you hate the mountains and the hills and are in love with beaches like the ones in Panjim peopled by Pessoa and all his other heteronyms that walk through the city in self-avoiding random walks tracing out the forgotten paths to memories in the labyrinth, which would make you think of endless mazes and how Borges would enjoy the people here, which would remind me of how Hedayat found his way to our shores washing up in Manto's Mumbai sometime after he had left it headed to oblivion, which would make me remember Muktibodh on his deathbed waiting for his first book to come out, which would remind you of Ginsberg in Kolkata as he wandered the streets befriending monkeys and the Hungryalist poets out and about the ghats with the dead and the dying, and I would wonder if Burroughs's wife really had to die for the word hoard to be realised, and you'd remind me of Hrabal, and instead I'd remember Verma in Prague writing in Hindi what Kundera wouldn't do in Czech for a couple of years, which for you really goes back to the letters Kafka wrote to the little girl who had lost her doll in that park that day all those years ago, but for me it is a another reminder of what Mekas said about the little things and the people and the countries that are forgotten, or was it Choukri, and this uncertainty would make you point out how Calvino showed that it's often unclear what or who it was that said or wrote or remembered or confirmed or erased something, and I would verbally agree and nod and hint that the conclusion is on the horizon except that my mind would be on the suicides, the slit wrists Keats or the hanged men Fisher/Wallace or maybe on Kawabata who gassed himself after being tormented by the spectre of Mishima of the katana in belly death, which always gives me that faraway look which makes you pull me back into something lighter like the time Wittgenstein advanced on a philosopher with a Poker and left after Russell's reprimand, and I look at you and smile a little and wonder if someday you too will get tired of waiting and leave me like that girl did Spinoza and if I should learn how to polish lenses instead, and I'd say something about the decade long silent vow that Kaufman took, and I would be a little taken aback when you'd mention that a woman set herself on fire in something Nagarkar wrote, but then I'd see the Buddhist connection of protest by immolation and grow quiet before pointing out that the escapees who killed the bodhisattvas last month or perhaps a long time ago were from a Pirandello text, and you would inexorably say that it sounds like there is an epidemic of such crimes, which would remind me of the people who died in the last one and you would express impatience with the way my mind makes the nearest and quickest connections when Nirala lost all of his family in the influenza a century before or maybe more causing me some annoyance that I would expertly hide by looking sincerely morose and point out the gradual collapse of all communication that was dreamt off by Dostoevsky in a fever dream in the cold of Siberian winter, and a part of me knows that you would take issue by raising Tolstoy and the need for gentleness with oneself above all in such times, and a part of me wants to agree unreservedly only that what comes to my mind slips out before I have a chance to consider the consequences and I have already mentioned Cioran or Baudelaire or someone that has made you shake your head in disagreement and sigh out some sentence that has Marquez's name thrown in which makes me lose the thread and wonder about Rushdie and how lucky he has been to not be shot dead in the street unceremoniously like Mahfouz I see that your eyes had darkened and realise that in my old inscrutable habit of mumbling my thoughts out loud I have said what I thought was private and now inflicted the gloom and doom generally isolated to the antipodes of my mind onto you and would almost begin an apology before say something about how Baudelaire would drop glass panes down from the third story hoping to freeze that infinitesimally small moment of joy into a small eternity which should make appreciate the everyday but would only serve to drive my mind to Yeats and his flattened circle of time and to be sensitive to you I would instead mention how Rimbaud had once bombarded pretentious old coots in Chennai before racing off with his co-conspirators and disappearing into the night and after what would feel like a self-similar recursive folding in of time into an infinity when you would so innocently inquire why we never mention any women I would bow down my head and become uncharacteristically silent.

The space of the real

It had been three days since the meeting. Karna was sitting on the small wooden plank placed on two cement blocks that served as the chai shop. Vikram liked this spot. He was on his second Gudang Garam, and Vikram was very late.

Karna didn't really enjoy tea, to begin with, but it had grown on him. Or rather tea drinkers had. The classes that they had to attend at this institute would end soon. He was almost always late. But the reasons that made him late these days were better than what they had been before. It was nice that someone had finally found a way to pull him out of his own mind. Something he had tried to do and failed. He decided not to ask for a third cigarette. The smog was already doing a number on him. Some of the students who were killing time inside the campus were already making their way out to the busses. The movement was constant. Not a minute to form a single coherent thought. Evershift nothink movement. He could see the dialecti-teach phil. professor sitting on the bench inside through the fences. The man hadn't been the same since Surf had killed himself. There was a growing incoherence to him. Without a counter-balance, he was beginning to spiral dangerously into those avenues of thought which led to incoherence and insanity.

'Been here long?' Vikram called out from behind him as he signalled the chai wala for his usual order.

'What do you think?' Karna noticed that he wasn't travelling around with a camera for the first time in years.

'Sorry man, just got caught up catching on some things.'

'Or someone.'

'Heh.'

'Submitted that short?'

'Yeah, just a few days ago. They'll screen the shortlist in a virtual viewing in a few weeks.' Vikram took his shikanji and lit the cigarette without changing hands. 'So, what did you find out at Algonquin round table?'

'They're definitely after whatever program it is that your girlfriend was a part of.'

'Hey, hey! We're not there yet.'

'Mmhmm.' Karna looked at the professor as he quietly opened his car and got into it. He didn't start the car. Karna wondered how long he was going to just sit there.

'Any idea how they plan on getting in?' Vikram sipped on the shikanji.

'From the sounds of it, they're already in.'

'Inside man? Sounds a bit out of their league to be honest.'

'I can't really say, most of the ones there were small fry. Hard to sift through what was true and what was just said to overinflate their own importance and knowledge of what's what.'

'Every place is like that. Sad to see the same things make their way into places that are supposed to be not about that.'

'The research, what did Neha tell you?'

'Almost everything she's going to say on the matter, I think. I won't go into what little she's told me about her own experience, but it looks like they're trying to perfect some sort of memetic neuro-programming.'

'Are they close?'

'Not by a long shot. From what she heard during her time there, it looks like a dead end. I don't know why anyone is really after any of it.'

'They believe it is real and close to working. That's enough for them.'

'I think I'm going to try and get into the complex.'

'To what end?'

'I'd like to get some footage from inside the building. Maybe even get some of the people who are working on the project on tape.'

'What's the point of doing that when you won't be able to use any of it?'

'Once it's out, It's out. Who knows, I may just put it out without my name on it.'

'I don't see what the point of going to that length is for a project that is essentially a dud.'

'Yes, but they believe it to be real. I think the fact that they're working on it is bad enough. Like we haven't already got enough social control and thought engineering without this shit in the mix.'

'I just think it'd be better to take some time and to reach some news people, try and put them on it. It'd have more credibility if it was better researched.'

'Nothing will ever equal the impact of seeing it on film. People need images, they need to see it for themselves.'

'Hmm.' Karna knew better than to argue with Vikram over the strength of sounds and images over the written word. There was no end to it, and neither of them had conceded any ground in all the times they'd gone over it. 'Hoping to make some change happen?'

'I don't think meaningful change is possible. At least not by anything that one person can do. It's just a small thing that I can do. If I could do it any other way, I would. Same goes for you I suspect.'

'That is a rabbit hole I don't want to visit today.' Karna took a drag and sighed out the smoke.

'You're too hung up on capital C change Karna. Just keep doing what you're doing and if something good can come out of it, it will.'

'Do you think we should say something?' Karna pointed at the professor, who had put his head on the steering wheel and was sitting perfectly still.

'It's not our place. Leave him be.'

'Hmmmm.'

He got up and paid the vendor. They started towards the buses.

'I think I might take some time off this month.'

'To work on your research?'

'No, I think that's a dead end. I'm taking a break from the blog for the time being.'

'There's no rush Karna. It's good to get some R&R in before the end sems. You could do with some time with Torsha.'

'I think I liked you more when you were a depresso loner.'

'Chal Chal.'

'Haha, who knows she might make a simp out of you yet.'

'This one's mine I guess.' Vikram pointed to the bus they were walking by.

'See you later then.' they fist-bumped and parted, going their own ways.

The space of the dream

The Chameleon and the Butterfly in the Desert with no name

The sun was warm on his back. The desert around him

stretched out in all directions as far as he could see. The green of the saguaro and agave with soft blues and wispy white clouds made their way to him. A man flew over him blown by the breeze here and there, letting the wind take him where it may. The swallowtail who dreamed that it was a man or the man who dreamed he was a butterfly dismounted the wind with a decisive flap of the wings and sat on the red fruit of the cactus. Opening and closing his wings in a quiet protest against loneliness. He sighed and moved to the part of his rock that had some shade.

He would have called out to the butterfly dreaming man dreaming butterfly but all he could speak in were hisses and sighs and sneezes, and felt it was better to not disturb the tranquil stillness and movement of his wing. He licked his eyes and wondered if he was truly a chameleon or a man dreaming a chameleon dreaming man. The meanings of lost cities and places made their way through him on his rock under the Sonoran sun. All he really needed was to eat a bug.

The space of the real

Navya weighed her options. She could apply for work elsewhere and wait out the privatisation. Things may land where they may. Or she could claim what was hers and move forward. That is what had to be done. She had to go public. Even if D.O.M.A. was nixed, she could always look for new work. She had been cracking her jaw and it had completely locked up now. She wiped the sweat from her forehead. One signature from some 10th fail minister and years of her work finished. Just gone without a bang, lost in the whimper of bureaucracy. There was no point in working with Credence. This wasn't the first time they had 'acquired' a department. What other alternative was there to consider? Wait to be buried in the footnote or appendix; asterisked out into obscurity. Her migraine began to recede as she decided on her course of action.

Once the general idea was out in the public, there would be many who would try their hand at replicating what they had been doing at D.O.M.A. But she had half a decade's head start. When they tried to shut her down, it would help her leverage her work with some other interested party. A part of her felt a tinge of excitement. All her life she had stayed within the lines, and now instead of toeing it she was about to squarely jump on to the other side.

The space of the virtual

Reconstructed Transcription of Voice recordings of one Nirava of Ajar Sting Ops. using a free speech-to-text service

Let's get the name out of the way first . . . speed . . . what bolt . . . no something better something hmmm Operation Savitr . . . should have coded it before but never got a chance on it because of how fast Anamika moved with it . . . touching . . . speed is the name of the game . . . so these accelerators these uh accelerationists incorporated these perennially online individuals some of them kids not kids but young and dumb at least . . . inside the notes provided by Anamika the Xerox letters with the symbols and the information on the symbology from source she is refusing to disclose . . . connection found by Nyra on some clandestine forum under the surface web frequented by these accelerators . . . so definite connection . . . the svengali needs to be verified before moving forward . . . Indian chapter of the organisation a motley crew of uni kids . . . not fully realised right wingers . . . . reactionary hyper centrists . . . not a surprise after the UNI reforms . . . organisation involvement all but a given . . . taking the direct route of the congress for cultural reforms this new Accelerationist Incorporated an obvious CIA front . . . end goals? Influence. How then. Bullseye on Anamika suggests D.O.M.A. linkup . . . information or espionage . . . revisit on the Credence announcement regarding D.O.M.A. in the company newsletter . . . put Vahini on it . . . source needed inside Department, talk to team about any links . . . confirm with Aruni on proper framing to avoid misuse by sanghis and propagandists . . . attacker lying low in Noida . . . considerable distance from the safe house . . . take updates from the tail tomorrow morning, revisit the budget later in the evening . . . amusing turn of events, cyclical everything . . . then aping McCarthyism to being puppets for the USIS . . . now aping Carlsonism and online alt-righters and back to being puppets for the empire . . . need to remind Nyra to ask that new intern to get coffee from that other place . . . good cup . . . affordable . . . need to investigate false flag northwoods ops. angle . . . unlikely in this case . . . not impossible . . . check in with Nath on the monthly spyware sweep . . . still reeling from operation winged horse . . . work with Aruni on the next draft . . .

The space of the dream

The ocean is always there in the distance. But the road I find myself on in my dreams leads to that one mountain that is the beginning and I fear may one day be very well the end. The cars change. I can never be sure what I am driving. But It's always me behind the wheel. And nobody else. The clouds that burst over the distance flood the valleys. But nothing touches the road. There is no water. No landslides.

In the passenger seat, there is always someone I know to be dead. Someone close to me. But in the dream, their death is the dream and the road to the top of the white-capped mountains is the life. The distance between what has happened and what will happen is folded in on itself. The road curves around the rock and slowly snakes its way to the top. I never reach wherever it is the road ends. It keeps pouring and when the ocean itself is drenched, the car falls endlessly and the dream breaks.

The space of the real

Anamika had seen the changes. It was hard not to. But there was something childish about men in their very core that made them keep pulling your metaphorical pigtails for attention. He was putting together the food for both of them. He still cooked like a college sophomore who hadn't had to fix himself a thing in life that didn't come in a packet with a spice mix. He had insisted on doing it and frankly, she didn't mind having a day off. They hadn't talked about the colossal fireball that their relationship had gone up in, and she wasn't sure if she wanted to revisit everything all over again. In her absence, people at the office had been covering for her but she'd have to go back sooner or later. This was a small slice of something that both of them had already let slip and sooner or later he'd say something and she'd have to refuse him yet again.

'You need to leave that on for a few more minutes.' she called out to him.

'How can you tell?' he had stopped with the pan tilted hallway into the plate.

'I can tell.'

'I was thinking maybe we order out now?'

'That would defeat the point.'

'Yes, but I would feel less like slitting my wrists, even if it is for half an hour.'

'Just a few more days and then you're on your way, I'm on mine and we can laugh about this when we see each other again in five years.'

'Just like old times.'

'You wish.'

He smiled and put the pan back on. She hadn't told him yet that the guy at her apartment was out on bail. Without either of them there to testify they had no choice but to let him go. Her boss had put someone on his tail, but she knew how much of a guarantee that was in the best of circumstances. One slip up and instead of writing the exposé, you are a footnote in it and you get a small column in the obituary section all to yourself.

'Here.' He handed her the plate. She looked at the dry food and thought about the little disappointments that she didn't even think about as they ate their dinner in silence.

The space of the symbolic

You know full well that seven people share your face. You know thousands more share your name. You know a million more share your ambitions and your hopes and dreams. Maybe a hundred million. Maybe more. That does not bother you.

Sometimes when you look at a laugh or a smile and the fleeting moments of sadness that they let slip unnerve you. You thought that you were sad and you allowed yourself to be who you were, but now this other person is there in front of you. Unmistakably miserable, but hiding behind a mask that you could never see through until just that moment. Now you're in a fix. Finding yourself in this Kabuki, unsure who is wearing what face and when. Looking behind the fox smiles and the demigod stares is harder than you thought it would be. Your stare is intrusive. The mask wearer feels their face go cold from its unwavering stillness. You can't help yourself. A part of you wants to know what their true face is, a part of you wants to know what your true face is. Do they see you? Do you have cracks that allow them to look into you? Now every eye is a dagger of light. Wielded carelessly. Now all faces in front of you are cracking and there is nothing behind any of them. The mask is all there ever was, for you and for them. Without it, the depth underneath is nothing but an unconquerable murky dark. You wish to erase this unhappy thought. But you know that it will always be a possibility that you'll stumble on it again. Now all you can do is reconcile yourself with your broken face. And look at the face in front of you and hope that you can help them put the pieces back together again.

The space of the real

Navya couldn't believe what she was reading. It hadn't even been three hours since she had given the interview to the streamer. The email attachment was on a joint Credence Industries/D.O.M.A. letterhead and was a letter of termination.

She reached for her phone and immediately dialled the Chief. No response. She dialled him again. No response again. The bastard was ducking her. She racked her brain. What were her options now? Fuck. There wasn't a second copy of anything. All of it was on her work computer. Fucking assholes. Should have kept a copy. A copy. Just one. This is what you get for being a goody two shoes. Stupid Bitch. It is still the weekend. She could be in and out within the hour. They wouldn't have gotten to any of the data. Not yet. And the techies are strong union guys, so forget about it until Monday at 10 A.M. All the work is just sitting there. She wouldn't need all of it either, just enough to counter the storm of bullshit that the media department was going to stir up against her. And those assholes worked weekends. Breaking and entering was the only way to go. No point in getting any of the Vehicles or Subjects to corroborate her story – any chump with opposable thumbs and half a brain would have no issues painting them cuckoo. No point in asking any of her lab associates. One or two of them might be loyal enough to keep their mouths shut but no way any of them would do anything that'd get them fired. Whatever had to happen had to happen quickly. She sniggered to herself. If there was any satisfaction to gained from all of this, it was a given certainty now that they'd boot the Chief as well. Her watch read 4:30. If the weekend skeleton crew leaves at 5 then she had to enter and be out by the time the janitors are done at 7. Simplicity itself. And even if they used the footage to stir something up, it would be too late. The work or at least the parts she wanted people to know would be out and there's nothing they could do at that point to undo that. As she locked the door behind her, she paused for a moment. Her heart was racing. She put her hand to her forehead, it was cold. Was she really going to do this? Yes, she was. She opened the door and got in the car. The engine roared to life. She zipped out of her grandfather's driveway and onto the main expressway.

She had the drive with her. Uploading everything to the cloud would have been quicker but she knew that would only make it easy for them to wipe everything off the moment they figured out what she had done.

The evening cold had already descended on the city. She hated driving in the smog. No going back. No point in going back. Her career was dead in the water unless she did this. This was going to happen anyway. All her interview had done was speed up the timeline. A pair of headlights cut right next to her and speeded on ahead. She pushed the accelerator. Most of the work wouldn't be reusable in any other situation but if she could get an MNC interested, they'd counter sue the shit out of whatever D.O.M.A. brought against her. This could work. She breathed in deeply as the glow of the Department building cut through the smog and made its way to her. Cool and calm. Cool and calm. She parked the car and killed the engine. Easy does it. Walk in and walk out. An hour and not a minute more.

'Good evening, Ma'am. Working the night?' She smiled at the guard as she pulled up her ID.

'Just getting a head start on things before the work week.' She walked in and started making her way across to the labs. The yellow evening lights were dialled down to the barest minimum. It gave her the creeps. The whole level was washed in an unsettling amber glow. She ignored the guy who was vacuuming the carpets and entered the lift.

She got out on her floor. Usually, she enjoyed being in the building after hours. The lab was quiet, and she was always glad to take any reason to not be home before her grandfather went to sleep. But everything set her on edge today. She felt like she was being watched. Her nerves were getting the better of her. Her system was just where she had left it. She plugged in the drive and started the file transfer.

The space of the symbolic

Movement

The way to hijack any motion is to introduce in the system another motion that can slowly and subtly change the original trajectory. There is no CRASH. If you are clever about it, people won't even notice something has changed about the way they are moving. There are some who will notice even the slightest perturbation and the signs and jitters that indicate the change in alignment but won't say anything about it. As keen as their powers of observation are, they fail to account for the compounding of the smaller effects.

Sudden breaks stand out. Crashes are a monument to a moment in time. They affect the flow of things and events around them. It is prudent to subvert motion than to halt it. Trajectories are meant to be negotiated, not decided.

The space of the dream

The sounds of the forest weren't bothering her. She could hear the animals moving on the branches above her, the million step marches of the ants and the tiny hops of the nocturnal critters all around her. The river was a constant white noise that helped clear her mind.

There was something familiar about the night, but the man in front of her wasn't. He was standing against the trunk of the tree like he had all the time in the world and nowhere to be. A glowing asp was wrapped around his arm and was making its way to his shoulder. The soft green light had sent the capuchins high up in their trunks and all the insects and worms had scuttled back into their crevices. She moved towards him, taking care to avoid the dried leaves and twigs on the forest floor. The glow from the light was the only thing that was helping her not fall over. The thin scattered moonlight that managed to make its way down through the canopy wasn't much use. As she closed the distance between them, the man raised his head slightly and extended his arm towards her, the asp began to make its way down from his shoulder and slowly inched its way towards his hand, towards her. The sound of the river was growing louder in the distance.

The space of the real

Vikram liked the eerie vibe of the semi-closed buildings. You couldn't pay for that kind of dystopian endless backroom cinematography. The janitor he'd bribed had taken the day off. He adjusted the camera on the cart. Excellent establishing shots. But he was running out of time. He had to be out of here before 7 P.M. He adjusted the button camera and pushed the cart forward, slowly. The first-floor hallway he was in opened out into the main hall below. Vikram slowly rotated the cart to get a shot of the chandelier on the ceiling. The marble polisher on the floor below added a nice unsettling hum of a background score to the piece.

He squinted at the glass doors. Someone was talking to the guard. Vikram slowly backed into the shadows. The door opened and a woman swiftly entered the hall, certainly not maintenance. The click of her heels echoed around the space. Something was up. He peeked over and checked where she was going.

Fuck, should have brought over the schematics. He quickly made his way to one of the elevators. If some shady shit was going to go down, might as well have it on tape. He'd figure out the context later.

As he walked out onto the floor the woman had gotten off on, he braced himself. This was the place. Neha had described it in detail so many times to him. He could see the file of people being led to the 'research centre' inside. He pushed the camera slowly towards the entry of the lab. Blue. Typical. The way she'd told it to him, this was the centre. He took out the camera and focused on the machine behind the screen. The chair was empty. But it looked threatening by itself. The scratches on the handle as people writhed on it. And no one complained. Because how could you with the NDAs they made you sign. The buttons were labelled – shit this would look great on the screen. He started the 'simulation.' The screens came to life with bizarre images. Vikram felt dizzy as he looked at them.

Slowly they began to form a coherent narrative in front of him. It wasn't all random. There was a rhythm to it. Narcotic fingers were tapping on the table regularly as a metronome, dup dup, quickening now the pacing becoming more erratic. The images formed into a man on the screen, heavy with the sickness of junk that attunes the senses finally to the real and the imagined going ons of the world outside and in. The man looked frenzied, paranoid. The image shifted from the outside to the cool, quiet, contented, chaos inside, the sick madness of flat hands shaking in the morning, shivering for a hit. Illegal auctions in seedy rooms, reauctions of the items that they'd themselves bought, thin bony fingers, and small stubby fingers dripping with blood. The man was lying on the grass outside now. He was watching the smoke curl through the shadow of a girl going to join the great smoke in the sky . . . dying flashes of fireworks in light and the paper making its way down in ash and smoke leaving the serene night fucked in its wake. The woman transitioned to flesh and blood.

Lying alone on her satin sheets, the ashes of her collection lying around her mattress. He had burnt down the paintings, every last one of them. He'd had enough, a small flick, a little tobacco ash and it all went up in the acrid smell of oil and canvas, hanging in the air, long after it was done. The image turned into flash of light and began to transition into a second story. Vikram turned off the switch.

Man, if this wasn't some Avant Garde shit. If the guy who stitched together these vignettes and AI generated phantasmagoria had submitted this to a festival he'd have won best film. But instead, it was here, being used to melt people's minds over nothing. Well, no issues, the work will be out. Just removed from the audience by the distance of one more lens. He turned around and got a final shot of the observation room. The woman must have gone into the other room. But from what he knew it was just computers. Did he really need a shot of them. She wouldn't know who he was. He could just pretend to be working. And let the cameras pick up what they pick up. A shot of someone working would add more to the film. And make it feel a little less guerrilla. Although that wasn't always a bad thing.

The space of the dream

The castle is endless. Not on the outside, but on the inside. All I see of her are the footsteps that she has left behind. I cannot keep up with her. The distance between us feels like it is encoded in the very nature of our beings. She has to run ahead and I have to follow her. I know the way out is at her heels. Sometimes I look at the doors to the left and the hallways that lead some other way – and I never follow them. I can almost see her leave the room as I enter it. I'm almost there. Almost at the outside in.

The space of the real

Pavan and Anamika were finally out in the open after days of being cooped inside the flat. He wanted to go out and see to his flat, but she had warned him against it. So they had compromised and decided to go out to a café that he'd never heard of, but was now one of her favourite places in the city.

The sun felt warm on his skin. He turned his head resolutely towards the sun and stared at it for a second. With his vision slightly foggy, he kept walking ahead – letting her silhouette guide him. He felt the deep idyll of the world around him seeping into his bones. The neighbourhood felt sleepy with everyone off at work and with school still in session. He followed her up the small cast iron staircase to the first floor of the building she had stopped at in the maze of the city.

He looked over the seven types of eggs and placed his order. She had already ordered without looking at the menu. The sunlight was entering through the left. They were just in the shadows enough that he could stick his hand out and reach out for the light. He couldn't help but look at her. Somewhere in the years between everything he found himself loving her the same way when they had first met. He realised that perhaps a part of the reason might be the novelty of having found something new in something old again. Or perhaps some idiomatic piece of wisdom that had functioned one way for all these years and was now working as the exact opposite; from out of sight out of mind to distance makes the heart grow fonder. And this small space between the two of them, here and now felt somehow more real than entire years.

'You should stop.'

'Give it a few days, and it may go away again.'

'And if it doesn't?'

'Don't things always do anyway.' She sipped on her coffee slowly. He was still waiting on his mint cooler.

'I like this place.'

'I debated bringing you here. Because I don't want to run into you here in a few months and see you with someone else.'

'I promise I won't bring anyone else here.'

Pavan loved how things existed in this halfway state where you had to share it with someone but didn't want it known too widely. His cooler came. He took a sip of it. A little too sweet. But not bad for the day. He checked his phone; his editor had reached out to him. He saw the link to an article. 'Have you seen this yet?' Pavan clicked the link and was taken to the popular indie news website. He felt a chill run through him. It was an exposé – about him. He skimmed the article. All of his heteronyms were laid out for everyone to see and all were tied back to him. He felt his heart sink. He would have to look for a new line of work. He forwarded the link to Anamika.

'Check what I have sent you.'

She looked up lazily, 'Is it a meme or something?'

'No, it's an article. Read it.'

He watched her expressions shift erratically through the spectrum and somehow, she became more beautiful to him in that moment.

'Pavan, I am so sorry. I had nothing to do with this.'

'I didn't think you had. Either way it's out. So no use being bothered by it.'

'What will you do now?'

'I'll cross that bridge when I get to it. It'll work out one way or another.'

'I'm so sorry.'

'Really, Anamika. It's okay.'

She reached across the table and firmly held his hand. Trying to communicate something important and urgent through this gesture. Pavan wasn't sure if he got exactly what it was. But he didn't mind. It was a warm and quiet afternoon and he felt a wave of peace go through him as he saw the waiter approaching their table with the food.

The space of the virtual

Making it inside Accelerationist Inc. wasn't easy. If you weren't fast enough they dropped you like the dead weight you were. If you went too fast there was always the risk of tripping dialectically into a flow of thought that threatened to shatter the uneasy equilibrium. One way or the other the hustling mechanism broke down who you were and if you couldn't keep up, well then that's just too bad. A lot of the members were always on the edge, but the rush kept it interesting. That's how you knew you mattered because someone else

didn't. The verses came in and went out – and if you were able
to catch the spot left on their way out then chicken dinner if not
then Chiba city blues.

The space of the dream

The obsolete smile of the being hung back in the air long after
it had vanished. 'I' could not move a muscle. All 'I' could do
was lie quietly in their bed and look at the incorporeal smile
suspended there, in the corner of 'I's room. This wasn't the first
time 'I' had found themselves paralysed. This ritual had taken
on the mundanity of everything else in 'I's life. And the being
was now nothing more to 'I' than another object to be walked
around. But there was something about the smile that resisted
interpellation. There was something in it that resisted reduction
into the mundane. When the smile was on the being's face
it didn't bother 'I.' It was only in the seconds after the being
vanished but the smile didn't that 'I' felt the true horror of what
was happening to them.

The space of the real

He had spent the last few days overseeing the production of fact
checks and counters that they would need the moment the govt.
decided to shift the blame off themselves and onto any and every
scapegoat they could find. The accelerationists were for the most
part dumb college kids who would need all the help they could
get the moment whoever was actually pulling the strings got

what they wanted. It wouldn't come to him as a surprise if some of them were culpable. Even if no foreign govt.s were involved in the clusterfuck, there were always some lines of action that managed to repeat themselves. The Nazi/accs always managed to find common ground with the Sanghis over their shared Aryan fetishes. Not to mention the wholesale imperialists who were always lurking amongst the L/accs or R/accs who were more than eager to launch crusades against corruption in the third world while buying designer lattes and vegan alternatives that funded their government's death squads in the developing world.

There was nothing that he could think of that would put them one step ahead of the modes of control. It was always that the catastrophe happened and they rushed in to try and patch the breaks in the dam. What bothered Karna more was if this was how it was always going to be. If this distance between cause and effect was somehow encoded into how the world functioned. Vikram's info would help but he was quixotic, to say the least when it came to sharing things from ongoing projects.

He closed his laptop and rubbed his eyes. He was on some level fundamentally tired of the loop that started with the people in power pulling some shady shit and ended up with people in his life hanging from the edges of cliffs that they didn't even know were there. His uneasiness floated around trying to fix itself on one point or the other. The whole edifice possessed a conceit that refused to be negotiated with. Small cogs in a big machine, no. Spare parts that were thrown out while the machine marched on. And if some gear or spindle were to malfunction or show signs of wear, then just reach into the endless sidewalks overflowing with scattered parts and find a replacement that fits. And if it doesn't then shear off enough metal to make it fit.

The space of the symbolic

Moonlit

In a dank rented room in a passive housing block built over convenience stores a man covered in weeds and wildflowers is putting pen to paper. The man is a snake oil salesman of the soul. He harvests the poisonous white ghost orchids that bloom in the once clean but now muddied waters of naïveté. He breathes the air through clenched teeth and doesn't notice the silverfish around him because they always eat around his words and never through them. The moonlight floods his little desk and he has drawn decades of life from the moon even as the young kick stools out from under them and fall to their three inch deaths on the strength of his words.

The space of the virtual

The room has not been in use for many decades now. It was an old socialisation program. It was where they congregated to discuss the things that they couldn't mention to anyone in the real world. It was meant to be a place free from the prejudices that animated societies in the real; the penumbra of all those doubts and doublethinks that lurked around every spoken or misspoken word. What the congregation never realised or at least what they never realised as a collective was that there was no way for them to be rid of the real. There was no virtual oasis that could free them from the desert of the real. For it was inside them, inside their minds that the real found its truest and starkest expression. It was inside their minds that the real was rendered into a meaningful whole. And one by one they drifted off and away from the congregation as the ennui of the real found its way into their virtual lives. As the misunderstandings and antagonisms multiplied between them, a little more space was freed up inside the room. And now there isn't anything left there for anyone to see except for pieces of old code.

The space of the real

As he entered the room the woman he had followed up to the floor ducked out of sight. Vikram wondered if she actually thought he hadn't seen her. He figured she wasn't supposed to be here either. Or at least was doing something shady. She was definitely on a computer. He casually pulled out the mop and pretended to sweep the floor. He was trying really hard not to whistle. He took out the camera and slowly panned it around. He focused on the various office bric-a-bracs, letting the camera linger on the mundane objects.

'What have we got here?'

Vikram's heart leaped into his throat. He turned around to find an old man standing in front of him blocking the doorway. He had a frenzied look about him. His eyes were red from a lack of sleep. Vikram slowly moved the camera behind his back.

'There's no point in hiding it now.'

'I was just cleaning the floor here. The camera is just a hobby thing.' Vikram felt the cold sweat make its way down his neck. There was no way he was going lie his way out of this one but at this point an absurd lie was as good a thing as anything that he could say. His heart sank, he dreaded the look of disappointment on his father's face when he would have to pick him from lockup.

'You're clearly not a janitor boy. So, who sent you, the fools at Edison, Inc.?

The man pulled out a gun.

Vikram watched the red spot slowly grow larger on his t-shirt as he collapsed on the ground. The man was standing over him. He knelt down and pried the camera from his hand and left. Vikram looked at the woman hiding under her desk. She was crying. He felt incredibly thirsty. He did not want to die feeling thirsty.

Vikram unclipped the button camera from his shirt and threw it to her, and then he closed his eyes.

The space of the dream

The fox looked up to his friend who had climbed up on the broken-down train. The bushy red tail caught the sunlight and sent it dancing over the snow. A part of him worried about his friend slipping over the cold metal, but the train was completely snowed in and it would cushion his fall. The electric wires over the dead carriages hadn't buzzed for years, since before the snow. Over the valley at the end, he was sure he had heard a vixen call out. His friend had fallen asleep on the sun warmed metal. He slowly walked away from the train and towards the call. Unbeknownst to him his friend opened his eye and watched his red bushy tail disappear in the snow before he closed his eyes once more against the winter sun.

The space of the symbolic

It had been raining endlessly for the last month and as a result many of the shops were flooded. Instead of trying to salvage the broken things, the shopkeepers had simply thrown the junk out on the streets. As a result, the road was strewn with old rusty typewriters and broken gramophones. The pages from old antique paperbacks had come unbound and were now lining the sewers. The first three days were the worst of it. The water never stopped during that time. But it was the worst time because people had hope. They had tried to swim after the pages and the Vinyls. But now that they had given up, things were becoming easier to endure.

The space of the real

Navya stared in disbelief at the dead man in front of her. The Chief had murdered him in cold blood. Her hands were shaking uncontrollably. She reached out to the button he had thrown to her. As she held it to the light, she realised that it wasn't a button at all but a camera. Navya disconnected the hard drive from the system and pocketed it along with the camera. She had to get out. He had left for now but he'd be back soon. She got up and softly began to walk around the body. Somewhere in her mind under all the chaos, she realised that with this she could fuck up the Chief's life. If he didn't murder her before she made it out of the building that is. The blood was only now making its way out from under him and collecting in a little pool. He was just a boy. She hesitated for a minute before bending down next to him. She patted his pockets until she finally found his phone and put it inside her purse. She wanted to get his wallet out but there was no time and she would have to move him to get to his back pocket. She closed his eyes with the back of her hand. It was an empty gesture but it was the only kindness she could do show him now. She figured the Chief had gone to erase the CCTV and would be back soon enough to get rid of the boy's body. She took off her heels as soon as she was in the hallway and made a run for it under the dim lights that stretched out in front of her. The lift was too risky. She raced to the service staircase and began to jump down four or five stairs at a time. Her feet hurt with every jump. She opened the back exit into the cold and foggy night. As she stepped out to the pavement a chill ran through her. She quickly walked to her car, the gravel biting at her feet. As she jumped in her car and closed the door she felt waves of exhaustion wash through her. With the initial excitement gone, her body went limp. She felt a strong desire to just recline the seat and fall asleep out of view. But she wasn't out of danger yet. If the man decided to rewind the footage by even a few minutes before erasing it, he'd be right behind her. And dying in a parking lot felt more depressing than dying in her office, but not by a lot. With the lights off, she slowly reversed the car out of the parking spot. All she needed were a few hundred meters and she'd be in the clear. She floored the accelerator and steered out of the compound and onto the main road. She had to call her sister and get her to move their grandfather. The Chief wouldn't have the balls to come after them as openly as that – but then before today, she hadn't thought that he had it in him to actually flat-out murder someone either. She needed to call the police. But not from her cell phone. How then? She'd have to ask Torsha. She would know someone. Navya breathed out to center herself and dialled her sister. As Navya heard Torsha's voice on the phone, she resisted the urge to throw up.

The space of the virtual

Scrubbing

Fastmin moved the cursor and saw everything that had
happened in D.O.M.A. The alert had flashed up as soon as the
old man had tried to erase the footage. Fastmin ground his teeth,
this idiot hadn't thrown a spanner in the works, but had taken
a sledgehammer to the gear assembly. As he watched the man
making copies of the research, he knew there was no point. He
quickly consulted the rest of the admins, and they all agreed. It
was best to wait for the girl. He typed out the instructions to the
mods and closed his laptop. The police would have him before
he could leave the compound. A bored researcher with a death
wish half a world across had ruined months of planning and
singlehandedly ruined his week.

The space of the dream

The cavitation created by the projectile disrupted the
surrounding tissue. The necrosis set in almost immediately
as the projectile passed through – crushing first, then lacerating.
The wave of pressure set off by the velocity stretches out
the tissue radially leaving an empty space. The red comes in
slowly, like an unspoken name that is communicated with
the movement of the eyes. It collects in a pool around the
cavity and then spreads out, slowly but deliberately. The red
moves over fabric and carpet and wood becoming inextricably
linked with them. The haecceity of the red is in its flowing.
The interruption of its laminar movement subjects it to a
temporary turbulence but the laminarity is restored as the

distance increases. The flow of red moves and covers the flatbed and then comes to an end.

The space of the real

It took Karna some time to understand what Torsha was asking of him. He had received a panicked call from her. But she refused to say what exactly was wrong.

'We need a place to stay.'

'And you can't tell me why?' Karna had never heard her this panicked.

'Can I count on you or not?'

Karna considered for a moment before answering 'Yes sure, come over.'

'We're already on the way. Will be there in ten.'

He felt a pit of uncertainty and uneasiness in his gut as he paced around his room. He shook his head and decided it was best to let her explain herself. His family would be away for a few more weeks, so it wouldn't be an issue if Torsha, her sister, and her grandfather had to stay for a few days. He set the kettle on the flame and went out on his balcony to wait for them. The evening wind felt cold on his face. The children downstairs were wrapping up their games or rather being forced to wrap them up as they were dragged back to their houses by their parents or elder siblings. Suddenly Karna felt extremely old and sad.

The headlights of Torsha's car appeared around the bend in the distance. He lightly slapped himself on the face and prepared himself. He had never met any of his girlfriend's relatives, and now he was about to meet all of them at once.

He took off the kettle and moved to the door, he could hear their footsteps on the staircase. Before she could ring the bell, he opened the door to find Torsha with two hastily packed bags slunk around her shoulders. He could hear her grandfather wheezing his way up the staircase. He took one of her bags and helped her in. She began to turn to get her grandfather. He stopped her and motioned her to get inside and settle in while he went to get him. Karna hated the way old people smelled. He slowly helped the man climb the steps. When he finally came inside – he saw that Torsha was already preparing the tea. He took her grandfather to his room. And told him he had his pick of the library while he discussed the logistics with Torsha.

'I wouldn't bother you with this if it wasn't absolutely necessary.'

'No, I'm just surprised that you trust me enough to come to me.'

'It isn't just that Karna. But it's also the simple fact that almost no one in my life knows who you are. So, he won't come to look here.'

'Who is he?'

'My Boss.' Navya said as she entered and closed the door behind her.

Karna and Torsha sat in perfect silence as Navya explained the situation. When she was done, they all looked at each other without saying a word.

Unable to bear the silence any longer, Karna turned to

Torsha 'All this time your sister has been working at D.O.M.A. and you never thought to mention this to me?'

Torsha hesitated before answering 'I knew what you thought of the place, and I didn't see what it had anything to do with either of us or our relationship.'

Karna suppressed his annoyance and tried to think what they needed to do. They would have to inform the police at once. And Vikram! He had to warn him as well. Karna took out his phone and dialled Vikram.

'Who are you calling?' Torsha asked.

'My friend is working on something related to that place. I need to tell him that a literal fucking psycho is on the loose, so he stays the fuck away from that place.'

A phone rang in Navya's pocket. She took out Vikram's phone, the colour draining from her face. Torsha and Karna both looked at her as the ring got louder and louder and louder.

The space of the symbolic

The Copy

The copy of the original was touched and loved and seen and thought about every day. The original was sealed in an airtight vault in an unpronounceable place that most people couldn't pull up in their mental maps of the flattened world.

The copy had foxing on the edges and although no one could see or remember how and when it had happened there were thumbprints on the bottom right. It could easily be seen that at some point it had been wrapped up in newspaper because of the ink marks a little left from the centre. Although it escaped many, some people managed to spot in the background faint words from the paper that were inscrutably pressed into the paint.

The space of the dream

The dizziness stemmed from the labyrinth of the inner ear. The severity of the vertigo rendered any sense of stability impossible to maintain. The inability to perceive changes in rotational and linear motion will persist for a few more weeks, pushing one's equilibrium to its limits until, one day, it ceases entirely.

The space of the real

She couldn't do anything but wait for him to say something. He was going through his friend's phone. He hadn't said a word since she had handed him the phone. She wished he would yell at her. He must be deliberating how to break the news to his friend's parents. Navya felt completely trapped and at her wits' end. She had seen someone die in front of her a few hours ago and the only one she could think of was herself. How to get herself out of this. How to get away from the look in Karna's eyes. How to secure her work. How to begin again. She knew very well that if Torsha had been the one in this situation, she would have been thinking about everyone but herself. Navya hated her for this, but not more than she hated herself.

'We need to go to the police.' He had stopped pacing around the room. 'We will give them your address and then wait and see how things go from there. If he tries to come for you then they can nab him.'

Navya nodded. Torsha was trying to comfort her by stroking her arm, but somehow her sister's hands on her body felt like she was being touched by fire.

'We can take my car.' Karna declared.

'There is something else.' Navya had just remembered the camera.

'Before he died, he gave me this. I didn't tell you before because it had slipped my mind.'

A look of recognition flashed across Karna's face. 'I have the connector for this. He gifted one to me when he bought it for himself, but I lost mine almost immediately.'

He came out with his laptop. Torsha and Navya gathered behind him to see what was on the drive.

A series of videos popped up on the screen. Navya saw the grey lining of her offices in the latest one. Karna opened the video, and the most horrible two minutes of her life started again. She had been playing it again and again inside her mind but having it laid out so barely, made her feel like someone had snatched the ground from under her. She grabbed at Torsha's arm to keep from falling over. On the screen the Chief had shot Vikram all over again. Karna was staring at the screen as the clip ended and the white replay logo appeared on the frozen image of his friend's corpse.

He closed the laptop. 'This is evidence. With this we have him dead to rights.' Karna was rubbing his eyes. Navya couldn't tell if he was crying or not. 'I will make a copy of this on my system and another to the cloud and then we will go and file the report.'

'Come, sit down with me for a minute.' Torsha led her back to the living room. And for the first time in her life, she followed quietly like a little child, holding onto her sister's sleeves.

The space of the dream

He could see the skull rolling down the valley. There was no reason for it to keep going. And yet it went on and on against the rocks against the grass and the mud and even gravity itself. The river flowed along for a little while hoping that it would meet her waters but seeing its stubbornness it turned a corner and went to meet the village while the skull rolled on. The landscape changed slowly and now without a slope it was almost impossible to keep going at the same speed and yet as it was possessed of a singular purpose the skull went on and on bobbing and weaving through the fields and the highways, cutting through the tracks and having close calls with the heavy tread of the eighteen wheelers on the highway. The asphalt had scratched it in a thousand places and chipped off even more. Almost out of teeth, the skull reached the sands where the ocean spilled onto the land and suddenly stopped, its sockets focused on the starry sky over the water.

The space of the virtual

The cycle resets every two or three years, and the same patterns of thoughts and sentences fly across the room. As the tiers are traversed the need for conversation decreases. It is common for a high-ranking member to say more with the move of a hand or a nod than an initiate could say in an hour.

The initiates are not allowed to see the Master irl. It is only for the Accepted, and even then, only in very specific circumstances. The initiates must first prove themselves to their local Capos that they are worthy of membership by going through the initiation rites that vary from region to region and Capo to Capo, but are an interpretation of the Master's creed.

The space of the real

The police had informed Vikram's parents. He was outside waiting in the car while the sisters filed their report. They were going to leave him out of it. Vikram's parents would never find out that he could have done something, anything. His friend was dead and he wasn't.

A part of him wanted to blame Navya. But he knew she couldn't foresee that bastard straight up murdering someone. A part of him wanted to blame Torsha, had she not kept things from him – Vikram wouldn't have been there. And a part of him wanted to blame Vikram, who did stupid shit and never thought twice before jumping ahead with both feet first.

Karna would have to visit his house. His brother would fly in. That is when they would hold the last rites. Karna felt an overwhelming sense of déjà vu as he remembered his father's death.

He was going through Vikram's files. Most of it looked like it was already put together, from what he could tell all it needed were the pieces that must be backed up on his home computer. Karna had no skill for editing. But there was no one else who he could leave this to.

On their way to the station, Karna had told Torsha and Navya about what he intended to do with the footage. Torsha wanted to object but any reservations she had, she kept to herself. To their surprise, Navya had asked him to leave footage of her in the film. Karna looked at the empty street in front of him and wondered if it was her way of atoning. Maybe something else. All Karna could see ahead of him now was a way to finish the documentary and release it for everyone to see.

The space of the virtual

The organisers apologised to the attendees when they couldn't get the director on the after-screening discussion call. The attendees were eager to see the new age director responsible for the short. The musician who was responsible for the part synth part noise soundtrack had assured them that he would get the director to join the call in a few minutes. Some of the people dropped the call eventually as the next virtual screening started. Eventually one of the organisers announced that the director would not be able to join the call and the attendees went away disappointed. Only on the final day of the festival did the organisers find out that the director had been murdered. A hastily assembled in-memoriam was tagged to the end of the festival program.

The space of the symbolic

The bright white light of the sun burns out the retina of those who unflinchingly stand with their heads raised to the sky. A different way of unseeing that finds its genesis in the annihilation in an overabundance of light and not in its absence. There is an omnipresent danger in turning away and shuttering yourself in the dark, for someone may shine a light and annihilate the darkness. But if one's capacity for seeing itself is annihilated, then with it goes the possibility of any surprises.

The space of the real

Pandemonium had erupted inside Anamika's office. The Editor was running across the small office in a frenzy. The journalists were typing, editing, cross-checking and tolerating the editor looking over their shoulder on a two-minute cycle. They had rushed to the office as soon as the video had surfaced. Everything had to be put out as soon as possible before someone else killed the story by getting the facts wrong. Pavan felt a shiver go down his spine. He hadn't seen a snuff clip for at least a decade. Anamika was consulting with the writers and went over everything before it was published.

The other people in the office were a blur to him now. He stared at her as she proofed the pages in front of her. He felt a strange happiness in his chest. She caught his gaze and he tried to smile. She shook her head and went back to her work. But he could swear that she was almost smiling. She muttered to herself while she worked. He had always liked that.

He knew there wasn't any point in him waiting and watching other people work. So, he got up and started making his way to the door, might as well stretch his legs a little or get something to eat. As she noticed him leaving, she shot him a look asking where he was going, he signalled to her that he'd be back in five minutes.

He had gone down the first flight when he noticed the man behind him.

'Make a sound and I will kill you first and then everyone up there.'

The space of the dream

'I' was sitting on the stage. Now in my fourth hour of talking to the people in front of me. 'I' was telling jokes to the people. The smiles felt strained. The lines under their eyes were deepening by the minute, but 'I' needed to keep on speaking. The world outside was closed off to all of them. The moment 'I' stopped telling his jokes the closed-offness of the outside would rush inside the small basement and all of them would trail off into their own loneliness again. So, it was important that 'I' speak. Not just for himself but also for them. Not that they knew it, or much cared.

The space of the virtual

This is a Memorialised account. It will exist on the internet forever to commemorate the life of the user. Soon the accounts of the dead will outnumber those of the living.

The space of the real

: It's finished.

: Of course, it's fucking finished. Fucking amateurs. I warned you from the get-go, not to stir shit up. But what did you do? This.

: It's salvageable.

: No, you dense fuck. It isn't. You're lucky he's not slashed up your family and thrown their parts out in the street.

: The data is still there. From what we can tell, they weren't as close as they were claiming to be.

: That isn't how the panel will see it.

: Perhaps not. But it is the truth.

: If you don't stop with that shit, I will bash your head in before any of them have a chance.

: And no confirmations on the whereabouts?

: You don't hand the keys to the asylum to the patients. There is no point in looking, so we aren't.

: Shouldn't we be all the same?

: To what end? He is finished. So is the whole unit.

: All the same. There is a chance that he may talk.

: Let him. Will help us locate him faster.

: I thought we weren't looking.

: Not proactively, no. But if a win falls in your lap after all this shit, then you take it. No questions asked.

: And what of the contract?

: They're still eager to push through. Not that they can stop halfway. No one wants to be caught with their dick in their hand. The other sub-departments are not insignificant. Even without the cherry and the sprinkles, a sundae is still a sundae.

: That's a relief.

: It should be for you. That's the only reason you've not been skinned and I still have all my teeth.

: I could use a drink right about now.

: That's the first good idea that you've had this week.

The space of the symbolic

The sky is falling

. . . and there's nothing you can do about it. You can watch it fall. And that is about it. You don't have to if you don't want to. You can look down, but make sure you're not outside. The shifts in the shadows might give the game away. The sky is falling and there is nothing you can do about it.

Sometimes when the clouds opened up in front of your eyes and flooded the small intersections and neatly maintained parks you thought to yourself what could be worse? Well, this is it. It was a long time coming but now it is finally here. The sky has been falling ever since you knew what it was to fall and what the sky was. It is perhaps best to look away. Or maybe it isn't. What do I know?

The space of the virtual

The virtual identity is suspended in its own inverted heaven over the others. It sees all, hears all but from a distance. It can see the others rolling the rocks up the hill to make their meaning; he can see the accepted trying to distil order and chaos into one – hoping this would lead them Up. It is not threatened by them, because they can never challenge it as long as they don't under-stand the importance of inversion. The virtual identity has its select circle and there are some who have themselves convinced that they are inverted and are in line to be the next, but in their heart it knows the sect will die with them. What will remain is a distortion that will emerge out of the power struggle between the Preferred. But this does not trouble it. All of this was an idea that they arrived at, in time, perhaps centuries from now someone else will rediscover and renew the idea by arriving at it on their own.

The space of the real

Pavan felt the barrel of the gun press deeper into his side. He started walking down the stairs with the man.

'You know, I dislike guns.'

'Yeah, tell me more.'

'We're going to look for a quiet alley and be done with you. But you know that already don't you?'

Pavan knew. And he knew that the man would have shot up the office just as easily if he resisted.

They turned into the alley right under the offices. There was no one around this time of day. He felt his heart sink. It was good, at least no one else would die because of him. Until at last the man found his way back to the office.

The man pushed him to the wall and asked him to lay his hands out. Pavan felt his heart rate rising. He could feel the sweat from his forehead trickling over his eyes. The stone felt soft under his fingertips. He closed his eyes and waited to be shot.

Suddenly he felt a cord around his neck. His knees buckled. He was gasping for air as the man pulled on tighter. Suddenly he felt a whoosh of air next to his head and felt the cord loosen around his neck.

He turned around and saw that the man was passed out under a broken pot and mud.

He looked up and saw Anamika staring at him in shock. Pavan felt indescribably happy. He broke into a wide grin. She returned a weak smile back to him.

The space of the dream

The whales were sleeping in the sky. The pod was resting all together. Mothers and Calves nestled next to them. They had dived in from the clouds above and were slowly drifting back up. Soon the sun will dip down and they will be up again, swimming.

The space of the symbolic

The finitude of strength, its limits define it more than the endless hope of its renewal or the ardour of the bearer. The lathe spins on and on wearing out the material, exhausting it. What remains may be the final product of the turner's design or a deformity. The only element that is writ in the action as a certainty is exhaustion. The ledger of blank lives grows and the only evidence to be given is the absence of those threads that bind them to the world, to others and to themselves.

The space of the real

This was the second time in three years he was at a funeral. Vikram's family were all huddled together in a corner. Karna didn't know anyone else there, and he realised he hadn't met any of his other friends.

When the time came for everyone to take him to the shamshan, Karna went in to lift the pyre but suddenly found himself pushed in between the guy who was lifting the front end and the guy who was lifting the back. He was the odd man out. He quietly stepped out and allowed the others to carry his friend to the pyre.

The space of the symbolic

Inner Rhythms

Complex behaviour implies complex causes. But that isn't always correct, is it? Simplicity leads to complexity and vice versa. The disruption of the rhythms inside the body and more importantly inside the mind inject chaos into the system, and the body and the mind struggle to piece themselves back together. The kanji peel off the paper haikus and fold themselves into cicadas whose chorus drowns out every other thought. The tymbal muscle vibrates and the resonance chamber mirrors the brain so precariously suspended in the human skull. And then it grows louder and louder until the nails want to scratch out the insides and pierce out the ear drums.

The space of the dream

The ever-living fire that kindles in measure and extinguishes in equal measure begins with a spark. The red horizon changes in an evershift of light and heat and sound and smell. It moves through all and is all. Slow and deliberate at the beginning but quick once it catches on. The red gives way to blue and white. And the wind bends it. The cloak of quiet protest and the breath of dragons as it consumes everything in its path. Metamorphosis, in the externality and internality of everything it touches.

The space of the real

Pavan looked at her face in the gentle embrace of the moonlight. Her cheeks looked soft against the darkness. Her nose twitched a little from the cold. The silence broke as she breathed in deeply. He lay at the edge of the bed, his eyes fixed on her. He had forgotten how it felt to be near her. Their hands hovered close to each other, yet remained apart. Her hair was messed up and as he tried to gather his thoughts, he realised that she smelled of summer. With a gentle push, he closed the gap between them and locked hands with her. She was lost in some deep unnameable thought. He more or less understood. He tugged on her hand to draw her out of her thoughts. She gave him a questioning look. He shrugged his shoulders and pulled her in closer. She grabbed his hair and tilted his head to her gaze. He stared into her eyes for a moment, before she pressed him against her chest. He closed his eyes and felt the ocean air on his face and the warmth of the midday sand on his feet.

The space of the symbolic

The loom sits gathering dust. The threads don't come together to weave a pattern anymore. But there is still work left. The threads and the needles will serve a purpose someday. The self that falls in pieces and trails behind in an effervescent comet tail of being and becoming will one day need to be gathered and stitched back to the body. If enough pieces fall, there stops being a self. And then these new threads that were twisted together from the intense light will serve a different but altogether important purpose.

The space of the real

'How far do you really plan these things out Navya?'

'That's not fair.'

'It isn't fair?'

'I put in my time Torsha. And now I am done.'

'Someone died Navya. Not just someone. The best friend of someone I really cared about. Does that mean nothing to you?'

'Do you want these to be the last things you say before I leave?'

'The last things I say to you before you leave for your cushy job in Europe that you leveraged using a death film, while leaving me here to put my life on hold to take care of our grandfather?'

'No one asked you to Torsha. Send him to a home. Go live your life.' She paused. 'Look I didn't want things to happen the way they did. Some horrible shit went down, and I made the best of it. I found the silver lining in the mushroom cloud and I won't apologise for it.'

'I have never asked or expected anything resembling an apology from you Navya.'

Navya embraced her and she returned her gesture half-heartedly.

As Torsha watched the plane take off, for the first time in her life she felt truly and deeply alone.

The space of the symbolic

Within the reach of my hands was that elusive sign that refuses to be signified. The white cliffs were waiting for the sunlight and I was standing there waiting for a sense of belonging with the world. In the oasis of my being with ocean out there all I could see was sand; the endless grains of the Thar stretching out to the end of time – a grain for every human sin. There were things that I had wanted to do but all of those wants and desires had been lost to time. The bliss of the everyday had overtaken the need for action. Only my memories are real. But every moment of remembering is once removed from the original moment. And in revisiting I had unknowingly woven in the act of remembering into that which I sought to remember.

The space of the virtual

The collection of guidebooks and travel logs carry detailed descriptions of places that no longer exist. Or perhaps they never existed in the first place. There are the words of the first wanderers, who on foot or by boat pushed on and found what had never been seen or experienced. Then came the second, then the third generation of seekers who had their own special means and were in the search of some specific ends and so too the roads they took turned and twisted according to the whims and the vagaries that drove them. White peaks and silent seas, stark deserts that meet the ocean on one end and the tropics on the other, all were logged one after the other. Many years later journalists and youths on their beaten down bikes and tired feet, clutching these accounts in their hands, could not find the places that were spoken of. The roads fizzled out, the hills ended suddenly before they were supposed to, the lakes ran dry and the ocean started before it should have.

The space of the real

Karna looked around the darkness of his apartment. His eyes moved to the green digits on the alarm clock, slowly adjusting to the dullness. The moonlight was reflecting off the yellow lacquer of the painting casting a murky glow all over the carpet. He let out a deep sigh. The ends of his life had begun to unravel, fraying out one after the other. He could feel them tugging at him in all directions, slowly pulling him apart.

He rubbed his eyes and shook his head – trying to shake off the lingering nightmare. He swung out of his bed and made his way to the kitchen. The French-press was already waiting on the counter. He put the grounds in and put some water in a pan. The sound of the boiling water hitting against the metal filled the tiny kitchen. As he poured out his coffee, he thought about his friend. He stepped out onto his little balcony and felt the wind on his face. The air was heavy with the smell of the ground after it had had some water to drink. The wispy clouds were travelling east post haste – dragging the stars with them.